CANDLELIGHT
Ecstasy Supreme

"DON'T YOU THINK IT'S TIME YOU TOLD ME WHO YOU REALLY ARE?" SIMON DEMANDED ANGRILY.

"I'm a—" How could she possibly tell him what she did for a living? "I find things," she finally blurted out. "People sometimes. I was hired to find your brother and get him out of the mess he's in. You've got to believe me, Simon. I want to help Paul, not hurt him."

"How can you expect me to believe you? Everything you've done and said to me so far has been a lie. Hasn't it, Jessie?"

She lowered her gaze. "No. Not everything. I meant it when I said I cared for you. I should have been honest, but I was afraid of what you might think of me."

"Well, I don't think too much of you right now, lady," he said in a cold voice.

CANDLELIGHT ECSTASY SUPREMES

NIGHT SHADOW

Linda Vail

A CANDLELIGHT ECSTASY SUPREME

Published by
Dell Publishing Co., Inc.
1 Dag Hammarskjold Plaza
New York, New York 10017

Dell ® TM 681510, Dell Publishing Co., Inc.

Candlelight Ecstasy Supreme is a trademark
of Dell Publishing Co., Inc.

Candlelight Ecstasy Romance®, 1,203,540, is a registered
trademark of Dell Publishing Co., Inc.

ISBN: 0-440-16404-4

Printed in the United States of America

First printing—January 1986

To Our Readers:

We are pleased and excited by your overwhelmingly positive response to our Candlelight Ecstasy Supremes. Unlike all the other series, the Supremes are filled with more passion, adventure, and intrigue, and are obviously the stories you like best.

In months to come we will continue to publish books by many of your favorite authors as well as the very finest work from new authors of romantic fiction. As always, we are striving to present unique, absorbing love stories—the very best love has to offer.

Breathtaking and unforgettable, Ecstasy Supremes follow in the great romantic tradition you've come to expect *only* from Candlelight Ecstasy.

Your suggestions and comments are always welcome. Please let us hear from you.

Sincerely,

The Editors
Candlelight Romances
1 Dag Hammarskjold Plaza
New York, New York 10017

CHAPTER ONE

Jessie McMillan quietly opened the door, stepped into the office, and closed it behind her. A large, imposing man waited for her behind an equally large and imposing desk, wearing an all-too familiar frown. She smiled in amusement.

"Practicing your Winston Churchill look again?" she asked. She remained by the door, studying him with her arms crossed and head cocked to one side. "A bit more lower lip and you'll have it down pat."

The man studied her as well, running a hand through his sparse gray hair. "Sit down, McMillan," he replied, continuing to gaze intently at her as she obeyed the gruff order.

This young woman was well known to him, through both past association and exhaustive research. Yet he was always amazed when he saw her in person. Her eyes, the color of aged jade, were brimming with intelligence. Shining black hair fell softly against her shoulders and the full, well-rounded curves of her breasts and hips outlined a beautiful body.

But her beauty was deceptive. This woman wasn't a fine porcelain vase, lovely to look at yet easily broken. There was an undeniable air of athletic grace about Jessie McMillan, an inner power and strength. That strength wasn't an illusion. Her past spoke of unusual talents and abilities, learned in murky dealings with people skirting the very edges of the law. All this existed behind a refined high-society image. A most remarkable woman indeed.

It was precisely this mix of beauty, brains, and ability that made her so valuable to Harrold Stone and others like him. She was so valuable that they all managed to overlook her irreverent attitude toward their high placement in various circles.

"Maybe if you started smoking cigars," Jessie said, calm under his appraising eyes, "they'd make you prime minister on looks alone."

"It wouldn't work."

Jessie saw the minuscule change in expression that constituted a smile from Harrold Stone. "Why not? I would think you'd love the chance to irritate anyone within fifty feet. Or are you allergic to tobacco?"

"No," he answered in a sigh. "I mean they still wouldn't make me prime minister. You have to be a British citizen."

"British subject," Jessie corrected.

"Whatever." He glared at her. "I didn't call you here to discuss political ambitions."

Jessie crossed her legs, arranged the soft silk of her pale-gray chemise, and fixed him with an innocent gaze. "I'm all ears." She paused, then added, "Sir."

"Why does *sir* sound like an insult coming from you?" he muttered. "We've got a very tricky situation, involving one of the largest investment firms in New York, a substantial amount of money, and a disappearance."

"Which disappearance, the firm or the money?"

He did his best to ignore her. "A man employed by this firm, one Paul Taylor, absconded with a quarter of a million in company funds," he continued, passing her a file folder. "In the process, he made some very big waves on Wall Street."

Jessie glanced through the file, then looked up suspiciously. "This is awfully sketchy. I don't see a police report in here, or even the name of the investment firm."

Stone nodded solemnly. "He didn't just steal money, remember. He stole a reputation. This isn't the kind of thing large, respectable firms want divulged. It's bad for future business. We're keeping this information as confidential as we can in respect for their otherwise untarnished business reputation."

"But how am I supposed to—"

He held out a big hand to cut her off. "The money was recovered, but too late to save the deal it was supposed to be used on. Not to mention the mud on their faces in a professional sense, Mr. Taylor's little foray into crime cost the firm a number of clients and a large profit."

Jessie nodded her understanding. "In other words, they want Paul Taylor, and they want him bad."

"I'm sure they'd love to get their hands on him, and according to our research they've tried. But *we* want him first, and we have every intention of succeeding where they have failed."

"But why the Security and Exchange Commission and not the police? I mean, this was theft, not sharp stock practices, so why are you involved?"

"In a way it *was* a stock scheme, but I'm not at liberty to discuss the particulars," Stone replied brusquely. "We need this situation handled quietly and quickly."

Jessie looked him straight in the eye, "I suppose that answers my next question, but I'll ask it anyway. Why me? I'm not a private investigator. One of the big agencies would jump at the chance to work with you."

"As you said, I've already answered that question," he said with an expression of distaste. "We don't need a bunch of overzealous operatives, scurrying around asking questions and arousing suspicions. No, thank you."

"And your own people?"

"Stretched to the limit. Besides, this is out of their bailiwick. We need subtlety, a low profile, someone who can get into this guy's head and weed him out, wherever he may be hiding. Someone who can convince Mr. Taylor to talk to us without resorting to force or causing heaps of unwanted publicity." He gave her the closest thing to a smile she had ever seen from him. "We need *you*, Jessie."

She sat back in her chair, thinking it over. It was just her kind of situation. Her reputation had grown at a rate that sometimes amazed her but didn't surprise her. There were a lot of people, at all different levels, who needed someone or something found and yet either couldn't or wouldn't go to the police or a regular private investigator. She *was* subtle, could think and act like a socialite or a cat burglar with equal aplomb.

In fact, she had very nearly become a professional thief at one time, and in certain social circles it suited her to encourage the idea she had indeed crossed over the thin legal line. The illusion of a nefarious occupation increased her

13

information network, broadened her connections in boardrooms and barrooms in the United States and foreign countries. And she had the added, very attractive advantage of being notoriously unaffiliated with any cause or special interest group.

"What happens when I find and finger this gentleman?" Jessie asked at last. She was looking at Harrold Stone very warily indeed.

"Jessie!" he exclaimed in a wounded tone. "We're not going to break out the rubber hoses and beat a confession out of him, so you can stop looking at me like that."

Rising from his chair, he moved his considerable bulk to the window and peered out onto the crowded streets below. He was silent for a moment, his broad shoulders hunched, apparently trying to decide how much more he wanted to tell her. Jessie waited patiently, a great many questions forming in her mind.

"Discretion is the key word here Jessie," he said at last. "It is entirely possible that you'll run into all sorts of strange things in your attempts to locate Mr. Taylor. At present I want you to report to me and only to me. The police may need to become involved at some point, but *I* will decide when." He paused, obviously troubled. "This stock transaction . . . I think something big was going on there, maybe even bigger than the firm was forced to admit. I want to know what."

She shrugged, knowing full well that was as much information as she was going to get—at least from him. *She* wanted to know what was going on too, and once something intrigued her, there was no stopping her until she figured it out.

"Okay. I'll take a stab at finding Mr. Taylor for you. Any ideas on where I might start looking?"

Stone turned from the window, looking immensely pleased with himself and the whole world. "Paul has a brother named Simon. The details are in the file. He might be a good starting place." He glanced at her, then made a pacifying gesture with his big hands. "You know I trust your instincts implicitly, Jessie," he said, "but I suggest you approach him carefully. We have no idea who might be involved."

She nodded thoughtfully. "I'll be in touch."

Jessie got up and left the office as quietly as she had entered, her mind already attacking the problem at hand. Simon Taylor. The file indicated he was a well-known sports figure, at least to those who followed championship karate tournaments. Jessie couldn't recall ever hearing his name before, but then she was inclined more toward ballet and the theater.

Eager to get out of the oppressive building, she strode quickly down the cool, brightly lit corridor, the sharp click of her high heels echoing against the marble floor. There were people in the various offices she passed, but the place seemed strangely deserted anyway. She imagined that if she listened hard enough, she would hear the sound of unfortunate souls strangling in corporate red tape.

She smiled at the irony of it all. The rules and regulations such agencies used to ensure conformity made her very nonconformist talents valuable to them. She was a person who could cut through the tangled bureaucratic undergrowth without calling undue attention to either herself or them, and it pleased her to be of service—for a price.

CHAPTER TWO

Simon Taylor lounged in the whirlpool, feeling the hot water wash away the last of his jet lag and loosen his stiff muscles. The white wine he was sipping was doing wonders for his disposition as well. He seemed to remember reading that it wasn't wise to imbibe while lying in a hot tub, something about the heat and the alcohol. Usually quite scrupulous in maintaining his health, at the moment he couldn't care less.

The phone rang and he reached for it, blessing whoever had the forethought to put an extension in the bathroom. He stretched and took another sip of wine before putting the receiver to his ear.

"This better be important, Barney," he murmured, thinking it to be his manager checking up on him.

Static filled the line, and for a moment Simon thought there wasn't anyone on the other end.

Then a familiar voice answered at last. "Simon? It's Paul."

"Paul!" Water splashed on the floor as he sat up. "How are you, big brother?" Actually, Simon was the larger of the pair, being more athletically inclined than his older brother. But six years and Paul's more serious attitude toward life made it quite obvious who had come into the world first.

"How did you find me?"

"One question at a time, kid," his brother's distant voice scratched out. "I'd read you were going to be in New York, then all I had to do was check all the poshest hotels." There was a pause, and when Paul spoke again he sounded less buoyant. "As to the first question, your big brother is in big trouble."

"Hang on a second." Simon reached behind him and turned off the whirlpool jets. "Now. Where are you and what can I do to help?"

"Believe me, Simon, it's tempting to tell you the whole sad story, and I could probably use those devastating talents of yours before this is all over."

There was another pause, and Simon got out of the tub in agitation, reaching for a towel. "Paul?"

"I'm still here."

"Where?" Simon demanded.

"I can't tell you, not over the phone. Anyway,

the less you know about all this the better. I just called to see if there's been anyone, um, asking about me."

Slipping on a robe, the tall, sandy-haired martial arts champion stood with his hand tightly gripping the receiver, increasingly worried by his brother's tone. "I've been on an exhibition tour in Europe. If Barney hadn't booked me for a tournament here, I'd probably still be in London for a much-needed rest. I haven't been in one place long enough in the last month for anyone to ask me anything," he explained impatiently. "What the hell is going on?"

"I just . . . I did something stupid, okay? Crossed some very important people. I think I can fix the mess I've gotten myself into, given time, but I'm going to have to disappear for a while." He paused again, then blurted, "Look, kid. I need a favor."

"If it's money, just name the figure, but can't we—"

"It's not money," Paul interrupted. "I knew what I was getting into, and I prepared for it. But there are some things, some papers, and everything fell apart before I could retrieve them."

"Are they at—"

"Shut up!"

Simon felt a chill run up his spine, and the hair on the back of his neck bristled. A feeling of paranoia suddenly gripped him. Just what kind of trouble was his brother in?

"You know where I'll be tomorrow night?"

"Yes. Let's make it by the red doors when it's all over and the crowd lets out. I'll find some way of contacting you."

"Good. I'll be watching for you."

"Don't look too hard. Someone may be watching *you.*"

"There will be a good many people watching me, big brother. And in case you hadn't noticed, I'm quite capable of taking care of myself."

Jessie made her way through the crowded auditorium, excusing herself as she climbed through a row of seats to an empty one in the corner. A lean, aristocratic-looking man waited in the seat next to hers, a scowl on his face.

"You're late," he said, leaning close to make himself heard over the multitude of excited voices. "And after you made me wait in line for the tickets. Honestly, Jessie, I don't know why I put up with you."

She settled her lithe form into the seat, then gave him a winning smile and a sympathetic pat on the knee. "We both know you do it for love, Miles."

He crossed his arms in disgust. "Love. Hah! What would you know about love? You have a heart of stone."

"Nothing so mundane," Jessie replied distractedly as she scanned the cavernous room. "Diamond, perhaps, or even platinum. But not stone."

It was an unusual crowd—a wide mix of nationalities and age groups, obviously having a good time, but not nearly as rowdy as boxing or wrestling fans. So this was the world of professional karate. Jessie felt the excitement touch her too, a pleasant acceleration of her pulse.

Miles tugged at her arm. "Yes, that fits. Heart of diamond and a soul of ice. Jessie McMillan, bounty hunter."

"You know I hate that term." She turned back to face him, her nose crinkled in distaste. "Except for very rare occasions, I don't even chase after bail jumpers. I find people and things that have been . . . lost, so to speak."

"Mostly men," Miles countered.

Jessie stared at him in surprise. "That's just because men get themselves lost more often than women. What's made you so belligerent this evening?"

Muttering under his breath, Miles settled back into his seat. He sighed heavily. "I don't know. I guess I'm just feeling taken for granted lately, that's all."

"Now, Miles. I appreciate you. You're a very valuable ally and friend," Jessie replied soothingly. Then she turned her attention to the raised boxing ring in the center of the auditorium.

The two fighters were warming up, trying to intimidate each other with the blinding speed of their karate strikes and kicks. It didn't appear to be working; both men looked calm and relaxed. Jessie decided the exhibition was more for the audience than anything else.

"Friend and ally," Miles muttered. "That's what they all say." He looked at her. "Jessie, I'm reasonably attractive, am I not?" he asked.

Jessie turned to him, trying to fathom his question and the petulant mood he was in. "More than reasonably attractive, Miles. What's this all about?"

"Then why do women tend to look upon me as their brother?"

She smiled affectionately. "Perhaps it's that protective streak of yours. You're a kind, warm man, Miles Delaney. The sort a woman looks to for solace and comfort."

"Bah!" He slumped in his seat. "I'm looking for encouragement, and you're telling me I'm comfortable. You make me sound like an easy chair or something."

Miles's love life had been considerably bumpy of late. It was, however, his own fault. "You just don't give a woman time to get to know you. You gallivant around too much. Maybe you ought to take up with a stewardess."

He raised his eyebrows. "Now there's an idea." Then he glanced at her cautiously, feeling the usual pang inside as he soaked in her beauty, a pleasing mixture of homespun and exotic. "Or I could take up with you," he added. "We have similar life-styles."

Jessie was well aware of Miles's longing glances. This wasn't the first time such an idea had occurred to him. "You're just feeling sorry for yourself, Miles," she said, taking the sting from her words with a gentle smile. "And we hashed this out long ago. Remember?"

"I know, I know," he replied with calm acceptance. "Why spoil a perfect friendship, right?"

"Right. Besides, you're not my type."

Miles indicated the taller of the two fighters with a jerk of his chin. "And he is, I suppose?"

Jessie turned back to the ring, her eyes intent on the fighter to her left. He was six foot two, according to the program she held in her hand. Sandy blond hair cut in a pleasantly wind-blown style capped his handsome head. She was surprised at his good looks. She expected him to be rugged, certainly, but not clean shaven with high cheekbones, strong jaw, and a fine, straight nose. Evidently he was as good at this as the program indicated, because that nose hadn't been broken, nor did the smooth planes of his face give evidence of his dangerous profession.

Dressed only in the loose white trousers of his

martial arts uniform, his bare torso glistened with perspiration under the hot arena lights. He appeared to be all hard, well-defined muscle from his neck to the black belt tied at his trim waist. Jessie nodded in silent approval at the incredibly masculine presence he exuded.

"Well?" Miles demanded a bit petulantly. "Is Simon Taylor your type or not?"

Jessie chuckled. "Oh, he's my type, all right," she muttered under her breath. "It's possible I'll enjoy this job a bit more than I should, in fact."

"What?"

"It doesn't matter if he's my type or not," Jessie answered, suddenly cross with herself. "All I need from him is the whereabouts of his brother."

"And if he doesn't want to help you put his brother in jail?" Miles asked sardonically.

"It may not come to that." Jessie was silent for a moment, watching the fighters gather their concentration in preparation for their bout. "I suppose I'll just have to convince him, won't I? By whatever means available to me."

"I was afraid of that," Miles commented sadly. "One way or another, you always get your man."

"Sssh! They're about to start!"

After the hyped-up introductions and some brief bowing to each other and the referee, the pair squared off. It was rather like a mix of boxing and karate, including padded gloves and fancy footwork. Those flying feet were padded as well, and the action much faster paced.

It was so fast Jessie had trouble determining what was going on at first. Miles helped her figure out the scoring methods, and her eyes educated themselves to look in the proper place at the proper time. Once accustomed to the speed, Jessie was hooked. Her voice joined those of the fervent fans around her. Her body moved in sympathetic jerks right along with the two combatants. Though she winced when a point was made by either man, she had already picked her favorite.

Simon Taylor was incredibly quick. More than that, there was a fantastic amount of energy behind every blow he delivered, literally knocking his opponent off his feet. Far from being a lumbering powerhouse, he moved deftly around the ring, maneuvering for position, fighting with his mind as well as his finely tuned body. It struck Jessie then that he might not be as easy to manipulate as she had first thought. Still, she was committed to try, and Simon was her only lead.

Then something happened that she hadn't expected. When it was all over and the decision came down, Simon Taylor lost the bout.

"No!" She found herself on her feet, booing the judges along with a thousand other upset sympathizers. "Are you all blind?" she cried.

Miles was embarrassed. "Jessie! Sit down, for heaven's sake!" He tried to pull her back into her seat. "He was off his form tonight, that's all. See?" he asked, pointing to the apologetic gestures Simon was making from the ring.

The crowd cheered him as he took his leave down a ramp to the rear of the auditorium, and Jessie cheered with them. "Did you see that?" she said when everybody had settled down. "He was sorry for losing."

"You expected him to be delighted?"

"But you could tell he wasn't just sorry for himself. He was sorry for the people who had come to watch him."

"Oh, sure. Saint Simon Taylor," Miles returned sarcastically. "Try asking him for our money back and see what he says."

Jessie turned to him and stared, then kissed him quickly on the cheek. "Why, Miles, what a wonderful notion." She grabbed her purse and stood up. "I'll do just that."

"Wait!"

She waved as she headed in the direction Simon had disappeared. "Thanks, Miles. I'll let you know how things turn out."

"I'm sure you will," he muttered spitefully. "Whether I want to hear it or not."

There was a security guard at the entrance to the dressing rooms, looking rather surly and unapproachable. Jessie approached him anyway.

"I'd like to see Mr. Taylor."

The guard looked her up and down, obviously coming to the conclusion she wasn't the average groupie. "Didn't you just see enough of him?" he asked, a crooked grin on his weathered face.

"I mean I want to speak with him," Jessie maintained, trying to edge through the door.

"Lady, there're men in there in various states of undress."

She winked slyly. "Why do you think I want to go inside?"

He continued to block the doorway but now eyed her warily. "Are you some kind of reporter, trying to break down the barriers against women in the locker room?"

"Can you at least tell him I'm here?"

That perked up his interest. "Does he know you?"

"Oh. You mean you don't keep *all* women out of the locker room, just *strange* women. Is that it?"

"Look, lady," the guard replied, his voice telling her he thought she was about as strange as they came, "do you see that corridor down there?" He pointed. Jessie nodded. "Go down there, take a right, then a left, and wait by the big red doors. That's the exit the guys use."

"Simon Taylor will come out there?"

"And anybody else you have your little heart set on seeing." He paused and looked her over again. "Of course, they'll be all dressed by then. Sorry to disappoint you."

She snapped her fingers, looked sorrowful, and went off down the corridor he had indicated. Parking herself against the opposite wall, she waited impatiently by the red exit doors. When at last they opened Jessie found herself staring into an absolutely devastating pair of liquid brown eyes. For a moment she couldn't seem to find her tongue.

"Hello," Simon said.

Open your mouth, you little fool, Jessie told herself angrily. She had talked with kings and kingpins, moguls and mobsters. On occasion she had been quietly baffled or respectfully silent, but never so bewitched by the mere force of a man's persona.

"Hi!" she managed at last.

Simon gazed at her questioningly, his head cocked curiously to one side. She was certainly a looker, whoever she was. Nice, shapely legs. Her sky-blue silk dress clung to her curves alluringly, inviting the eye upward to the gentle swell of firm breasts and her delicately arched throat. Though she had an aristocratic bearing, her face was more on the American wholesome side of pretty. And those eyes! He didn't know what she was doing there, but he could look into those eyes forever—or at least until she told him what she wanted.

"Something I can do for you?" he asked.

You can tell me where your brother is, she thought. But she was well aware she couldn't just come straight out and ask him, at least not until she knew the extent of his involvement, if any.

"I was wondering if . . ." She trailed off, still having trouble concentrating on the matter at hand. He was looking at her in the most intriguing way.

"Oh." Simon nodded knowingly, and took a ballpoint pen from his shirt pocket. He smiled graciously, his eyebrows arched. "Though I don't know why you'd want my autograph after the terrible performance I put on tonight."

Finally Jessie's mind started working again. Though tempted to call him conceited and stalk off, that was hardly the way to win his confidence. And she had to look at it from his point of view. There she was, waiting for him outside the dressing-room door and acting like a star-struck teenager. It would be better to play along.

She fumbled in her bag, came up with a small, spiral-bound notebook, and handed it to him. "I thought it was a bad call by the judges," she said honestly.

His smile turned into a broad grin. "A woman after my own heart. Honestly, though, the judges were right. I was weak, and I had trouble concentrating."

"You call that weak?" Jessie replied, having no trouble sounding incredulous.

"Are you a student of the martial arts?"

"Well, no," she admitted. Though she had picked up a few interesting moves in her varied career. "This is the first tournament I've attended."

"I see." Simon frowned, puzzled by this lovely woman who wasn't a student, or a fanatic fan, and yet had taken the trouble to seek him out. But she was smiling at him, and his frown disappeared. "I meant my technique was weak. The power was there, but the execution was lousy. There's a lot of hype surrounding sport karate, but it still has its roots in the physical art form. Hence my low scores."

Jessie decided to try a bit of blatant flattery. "I don't know. I thought your form was quite nice."

Initially startled, Simon then broke out laughing. "I hope you come to all my bouts, especially the ones I lose." He took another flickering glance at her feminine attributes. "You have a pretty nice form yourself."

"Think I could be a contender?" she asked slyly, playing the moment for all it was worth.

"Definitely." Simon had no idea what was going on there, but whatever the motive, he certainly wasn't about to turn away from this lavish attention. "How shall I make this out?"

"Excuse me?"

He held up her notebook. "To . . ."

"Oh." Jessie fought a very unaccustomed blush. Maybe she had been playing a role, but she liked it. "To Jessie."

Simon wrote in the notebook for a moment, then gave it back to her, his hand brushing hers. She was surprised by the touch, thinking his skin would be tough and calloused. But he had nice hands, big, capable, and well formed. She read the autograph aloud.

"To Jessie, the most beautiful liar I've ever met." Her eyes flashed to his for a moment, seeing only innocent amusement. She continued, "From your fan, Simon Taylor."

"Okay?" he asked.

"Perfect." She sensed the moment slipping away now that her reason for being there had been ostensibly taken care of. Somehow she had to keep things going. "I was supposed to ask you a question. I came with a friend who was less impressed with your performance than I was."

"Ask away."

"He wanted to know if he could get his money back."

"And just where is this friend?" Simon asked, his voice full of threat but his brown eyes shining with playfulness.

Jessie laughed. "Already gone, lucky for him."

"And for me too." Simon liked her laugh, and the way she tossed her shoulder-length black hair with an inviting movement of her head. "I'm not in the habit of making restitution to unappreciative patrons. You, on the other hand, are a different story entirely. This was the first tournament you've ever attended, you said?"

"Yes." *I've got you now, Simon Taylor,* Jessie thought. The idea pleased her for more reasons than the opportunity to question him about his brother. "But I had a very nice time."

It was true. She had enjoyed the match more than she thought she would. She was also enjoying talking to him more than she probably should, but what the heck. In her line of work, it wasn't often she had a chance to have fun and work at the same time.

"Still, your first tournament and all." He rubbed his smooth jawline with one hand, frowning with mock deliberation. "Surely we could come up with some way to make it a more pleasurable memory."

There was a hint of sensuality in his voice that made Jessie wonder if she hadn't overdone it a bit. After all, he was a big man, and she didn't know him at all. But she decided she'd play out the hand. She didn't really have much choice. At the moment he was her only link to Paul Taylor.

32

"What do you have in mind?" she inquired at last.

He had a number of things in mind, but this situation still seemed a bit strange to him. Contrived, perhaps. He shrugged the feeling off, knowing he was still paranoid from his brother's odd phone call.

"How do you feel about late suppers?"

"They're the best kind," Jessie replied, breathing an inner sigh of relief.

Simon hesitated for a moment, glancing at his watch. Paul had said he would make contact after the tournament was all over and the crowd began to leave. That wouldn't be for at least two hours yet, what with the lengthy program planned for this evening. Plenty of time for a good meal in the company of a beautiful and interesting woman.

"Good. There's this marvelous seafood restaurant at Forty-fifth and Madison," he said, linking his arm through Jessie's.

There was a solid feel to his arm, a pleasant warmth emanating from his body. Jessie was trying to keep her mind on business, but it wasn't easy.

"I know the place. I can taste that Creole rice now."

"Me too."

Laughing, they strolled from the building arm in arm. It had occurred to Simon that perhaps

33

this unusual woman—and the somewhat suspicious way he had met her—might have something to do with his brother. He supposed she could even be some kind of go between, since Paul seemed so worried about being overheard or seen.

He would just have to play it by ear. Once away from the auditorium, she might come clean and reveal the real reason she had been waiting for him. Or maybe she was just what she appeared to be, an intriguing woman who had been taken by his style. He was certainly taken by hers, so either way this impromptu date was anything but a hardship.

His next step therefore depended on what happened with Jessie. If she was simply an interested fan, he would come back later and see if Paul was anywhere about. *Of course*, he thought with an undeniable anticipation, *after I find out what Paul wants me to do, I'd still have time to find out even more about the beautiful woman at my side.*

Their waiter was attentive and the food just as marvelous as they both remembered. Jessie noticed a tension in Simon, a certain uneasiness, and therefore kept the conversation light. It wasn't difficult; she felt quite comfortable in his company.

"This isn't fair, you know," Simon remarked.

"Here I am, buying you dinner because *I* lost a match, and I don't even know your last name."

Jessie grinned. "Next time you'll win, and I'll buy. It's McMillan."

"Scottish?"

"I suppose," she replied with a shrug. "I consider myself plain old American. I doubt there's any royal blood in my veins."

Simon studied the soft curves of her face and the way the light made her midnight-black hair shine. There wasn't anything plain about her. "Oh, I don't know. You have a definite regal air about you."

"Thank you." He was a charmer, this unusual man. A blend of warrior and gentleman. "Just how does one get into the, um, profession you're in?"

"It does look rather odd on credit applications," he said, his broad shoulders shaking with a deep, pleasant chuckle. "Occupation: Knocking people down."

"Seriously."

"I started training when I was seventeen. A rowdy kid with nowhere to go at night who wanted to learn how to fight," Simon began. "Strangely enough, though, from the moment I walked into the *dojo* the fighting part started slipping into the background. There was so much to learn, and the workouts were very

35

hard. At first I didn't have the energy to get into trouble, and then I lost interest in even trying."

A frown furrowed her brow. "So why—"

"Did I start fighting professionally?" Simon completed. "Money. Fame and recognition. I turned pro in college, because I was a horrible student and wanted to be doing at least one thing I was good at," he explained. "The dean was furious because I could no longer compete for the school. I think I graduated mainly because he wanted to get rid of me."

From her research, Jessie knew better. Simon Taylor hadn't been an honor student, but he had been in the top fifty percent of his class at a fairly large midwestern university. He wasn't dumb. Like his elder brother, he had majored in business. Paul Taylor, of course, had gone on for an MBA then into the world of stocks and bonds. Even so, she would say Simon was still the smarter of the two, considering the trouble Paul had gotten himself into.

"I read in the tournament program that you operate a chain of karate schools," Jessie said. "Is that a major interest or just diversification?"

"Both," he replied, looking at her speculatively. Why did he have this odd feeling she knew more about him than she was telling? "As well as a retirement program. As with any other professional athlete, my career as a participant is limited. There's only so long one can take the pounding."

"Or would want to," Jessie noted. "Still, you seem to be holding up fairly well."

Simon smiled at the laughter in her eyes. "I've got a few years left in me. I've been a champion before, and I'm on the comeback trail, tonight's loss notwithstanding. Prospective students see my name on the school door and know I can deliver what I promise."

"Championship titles?"

"Same old hype." He shrugged. "They come in to learn how to fight and walk away with more of an education than they bargained for. But I have some students here and there who show great promise. It takes a tremendous amount of drive and dedication."

"And tough ribs, I would imagine," Jessie remarked.

"That too."

They laughed, and sipped at their after-dinner drinks. Simon was having a good time, but still had a feeling there was more there than met the eye. He had given up on the idea that Jessie was sent by his brother. It would have been a nice gift from Paul if he had sent this lovely woman to contact him, but she would have said something by now if that was the case.

So what was she after? He wanted to think she was after *him*, because he was quite taken with

Jessie McMillan. But she could be one of the people Paul had crossed, or someone sent by them to see if he knew where Paul was.

"What line of work are you in, Jessie?" he asked in a casual tone.

No, Jessie thought, *he certainly isn't dumb.* She could tell he liked her, but could also tell by the intensity of his gaze that he was suspicious of her too. Why shouldn't he be? She had appeared out of nowhere, with no clear intention other than meeting him. It would be interesting to tell him she was an investor, just to see his reaction. But she had already decided on what role to play.

"I'm a collector, of sorts," she said with an enigmatic smile. "Antiques, paintings, jewelry. Acquire here, sell there at a profit." She paused, her lips pursed, apparently trying to decide something. "I suppose I should really tell you the truth now, shouldn't I?"

Simon's eyes widened, and he stared at her blankly for a moment. "Please do," he said at last.

This was where Jessie's research would prove itself. She hoped she had her information straight. "Don't take me wrong. I did enjoy the tournament, and dinner was marvelous. But I'm not the autograph hunter I appeared to be."

"I never thought you were," he said flatly. "Go on."

Jessie took a deep breath. "I hear you have something of a collection yourself. Japanese armor and weaponry, swords of the samurai and such. I had hoped to interest you in a *Katana* I may be able to get my hands on. The great sword of a court official during the Tokugawa Shogunate."

For a moment Jessie thought she had gotten it wrong or had been misled as to the availability of such a weapon. Such was the dark, brooding frown Simon was giving her.

Then he tipped back his head and laughed, and her worry turned to laughter as well when he nearly fell off his chair. "You really had me going there for a minute, Jessie McMillan," he managed at last. "If you only knew . . ." He trailed off, still chuckling.

"I take it you're not interested?" she offered with chagrin. Her ploy had worked. She could practically feel the tension draining out of him.

He shrugged, a carefree gesture of indecision. "I might be. I don't buy just any piece of wood and steel. My collection is pretty well rounded out, but I'm always on the lookout for a real find." Simon looked at her, seeing her in a new light and finding himself more attracted to her than ever.

This was the tricky part. She needed to get more involved in Simon's life, but had grown to like him enough not to lead him on. There was a glimmer of desire in his eyes, and she had no doubt the same glimmer was apparent in her own. But he wasn't aggressively on the make, and she could handle this mutual attraction developing between them without either of them getting carried away.

"Perhaps if I could arrange to see your collection," she said thoughtfully, "and compare the quality, I would know if it's worth my time and yours to show you the sword."

There was just enough of a businesslike quality to her voice to make Simon push aside his hopes for a passionate conclusion to this unusual evening. Still, one never knew what might develop, and he had an ace up his sleeve.

"As a matter of fact, I had some of my collection with me on the European tour I just returned from. The pieces are in my room at the Plaza." Signaling for the check, he paid it then turned back to her, noticing her uncertain frown. "I thought you wanted to sell me a sword?"

Jessie's bravado had faltered. Simon's home was in Texas, and she had assumed his collection would be there. She had also hoped Paul Taylor was at Simon's home too, and that Simon would be reluctant to arrange a showing. Now what?

She had to get information out of him, get him to talk about his brother. There were a lot of unanswered questions, but his hotel room didn't seem the best place to ask them. She was very much aware of the chemistry between them.

When in doubt, change the subject. "European tour?" Jessie asked innocently.

Simon nodded, an amused grin tugging at the corners of his mouth at her obvious ploy. "I've been traveling over there for a month. Probably accounts for my loss tonight, in fact. I told my manager I needed a rest."

Though he tried to contain it, his grin slowly became a wide, knowing smile. It seemed he had finally broken through that calm and collected exterior of hers to discover the barest hint of womanly uncertainty.

Jessie was struck with a disturbing thought. Since he hadn't even been in the country, Simon might know less about this whole affair than she did. The best thing would be to try to keep an eye on him and at the same time keep clear of his tempting grasp.

"And here I am keeping you up late," she remarked.

Simon looked at his watch and found he had lost track of time in her pleasant company. "As a matter of fact, I do have other obligations this evening," he said. He took her hand and stood up, grinning apologetically. "I'll hail a cab and drop you off—"

"That's all right," Jessie interrupted. His sudden haste gave her a hunch as to what his other

41

obligation might be. "I think I'll sit here and enjoy the last of my coffee. Thank you for a lovely dinner."

"Perhaps we could have breakfast together tomorrow in my suite and see if we'll be able to do business," he said, letting go of her hand with great reluctance. "How does that sound?"

Jessie smiled at her good fortune. Breakfast was much safer than a nightcap in his room. "It sounds just fine. I'll give you a call in the morning."

"I'll be waiting to hear from you. Good night."

"Good night." She watched him leave the restaurant and waved as he got in a cab and took off. The cab she hailed a moment later stayed a discreet distance behind as per her instructions.

She had better watch her step with Simon Taylor. She was already so attracted to him, found herself liking him so much she couldn't believe he could be involved in anything shady.

Making that kind of an assumption at this early stage of her investigation was not only premature, it could be hazardous. It was important to stay objective, remember to ask the right questions, and stop getting caught up in the parade of lovely fantasies running through her head.

CHAPTER THREE

To Jessie's surprise, Simon went straight back to the arena. She had the cabdriver drop her off a block away and walked the rest of the way. She entered the building using her ticket stub and started looking around, keeping herself hidden in the dense crowd.

A mock sword battle was being fought in the ring, the sharp clack of the wooden blades on plastic armor giving the throng great reason to cheer. Jessie ducked into one of the side corridors to escape the noise.

Why would Simon go back there? He had seemed about to leave when she had accosted him earlier at the dressing-room doors. Perhaps whatever business he had there was going to take place by those red doors. She hoped so. If he was hidden among the crowd she probably wouldn't be able to spot him, though he might very well spot her if she kept wandering around.

43

She didn't want to lose him, but she didn't want to spook him at this early stage either.

Down the corridor she found a connecting hallway and went into it, making her way vaguely in the direction of the dressing rooms. She came out into another corridor and looked around, congratulating herself on locating the correct spot. There were the doors, and there was Simon, his back to her as he looked expectantly up the corridor toward the main auditorium. Jessie ducked back into the hallway and waited.

She didn't have to wait long. People started pouring through the exits, talking and gesturing cheerfully, filling the corridor with a growing wall of noise. She kept her eyes on Simon.

Several people recognized him, and he impatiently signed autographs, not being rude but not encouraging much conversation either. It didn't do much good, for soon there was a circle of people around him. Most were male, though he did have his share of female admirers. Jessie noticed that most were young—except for one man off to the side.

The man had on a baseball cap, jeans, and a jersey-style shirt with METS on the back. He seemed to be hanging back, waiting for a chance to speak to Simon, though Simon hadn't noticed him yet. Through the crowd, Jessie was just able to make out a fringe of grayish-blond hair at the back of his head. There was something about him, something vaguely familiar, and she felt a surge of excitement.

Making her way back up the corridor was like swimming against the current of a river, with every step forward through the crowd taking her two steps back. The more she fought, however, the more certain she became that the man standing next to Simon now was none other than her quarry, Paul Taylor. She had no idea what she would say to him when she reached him, but this was an unbelievably lucky break and she was determined to grab it.

Then someone grabbed *her.* She turned, furious, and glared at the thin man impeding her progress. "Let go!"

"What's going on?" Miles asked, his hand still clamped onto her arm. "I saw you come back and got worried. What—"

"Let go!" Jessie cried again. "That's the man, that's Paul Taylor!" She turned just in time to see him put something in the pocket of Simon's suit coat. Simon was being buffeted so much by the excited throng around him he didn't seem to notice.

Breaking free of Miles's grasp, Jessie redoubled her efforts, only to watch the man in the METS shirt slip into the crowd and away from her in the other direction. Going with the crowd, he was swept far out of her reach in a matter of seconds, and out of sight a few seconds after that. Miles, too, was being swept away.

Frustrated, she called out, "Stop that man!"

Several people turned and looked at her, but it was a New York crowd, wise to the ways of a quickly moving mass of people and the very real possibility of getting trampled should they stop in their tracks.

Jessie turned abruptly and started back the way she had come, finding the going much easier until again a hand clamped onto her arm. This hand, however, was big, muscular, and inescapable.

"What are you doing here?" Simon asked, the dark suspicion in his voice echoed in his eyes.

"That man," she said, thinking quickly and pointing toward the square of night sky marking the exit, "I think he stole your wallet."

Simon stared at her doubtfully, then patted his pockets, still keeping a firm grip on her arm. "No, I . . ." He trailed off, having found whatever it was the man had so stealthily given him. He didn't bring it out of his pocket. Instead he scanned the exiting crowd with an anxious expression. "What man? Where?"

"He's gone," Jessie said dejectedly. She had made two mistakes. One, she had let Paul Taylor —she was certain it had been he—escape right out from under her nose. Two, she had made Simon aware of whatever his brother had given him. If she had kept quiet about it, she could have picked his pocket and maybe gotten another lead. Impossible now; Simon had his hand firmly wrapped around whatever it was.

Dragging her with him, Simon drove through the crowd like an arctic icebreaker, out into the cool night air and the relative freedom of the sidewalk. But he knew it was a futile gesture. Paul would be blocks away by now.

"Damn," he muttered. Then he turned and looked at the prize he still held. "What are you doing here?" he demanded again, frustration making his voice rough. His brown eyes were full of accusation.

She felt angry and frustrated herself, but couldn't afford the luxury of telling him she'd go where she pleased. He was her only contact and now doubly important; in his hand she saw a small notebook like the one he had autographed for her earlier.

But this wasn't an autograph hound's treasure. It was a communique from the man she had been hired to find. A man she'd had within her grasp and let slip away.

"What are you so angry for?" she asked innocently. "I came back to catch the rest of the show, that's all."

Simon glared at her, trying to make up his mind whether to believe her or not. "And just conveniently interrupted a pickpocket?"

He's lying, Jessie thought. That meant he did know what was going on. From the anxiety he had shown when he went after his brother, she didn't think he knew where Paul was, but he still might know the best places to look. Or perhaps the notebook would tell him.

"I was on my way out when I saw you at the doors where we met," she replied, trying to get his mind off of the last few minutes and back on the pleasant dinner they had shared. "I was trying to make my way through your admirers when I saw that guy with his hand in your pocket." Jessie looked at the hand he still had clamped on her arm. "I'm sorry I tried to warn you."

"No," he said with a sigh. He released her, more confused than ever. "I'm sorry. I thought I —I thought I knew the guy. My mistake."

"Then he didn't steal anything?"

Simon reached into his inside coat pocket to get his wallet. When he took it out, the notebook was no longer in his hand. "All safe and sound. See?"

"Good," Jessie said, trying not to let her surprise show. *Very good,* she thought. With his quick hands, he would make a pretty good pickpocket himself. As she watched him fold his arms across his broad chest, she knew she would have little chance of lifting the notebook without his knowing it.

Unless, of course, she got him to take off his coat. Her mind clamped down on the thought. She didn't work that way, never had and never would. Still, with this man, and in view of the undeniable attraction she had for him, the idea was rather tempting. Again she had to brush off another, slightly more erotic thought. *Business, Jessie,* she told herself. *Stick to business.*

"Still up to our business breakfast tomorrow?" she asked, reminding herself as well as Simon as to the nature of their relationship. "I still want to sell you that sword."

"How about a nightcap right now?" Despite the suspicions still plaguing him, he was still very much drawn to this mysterious woman. "We could mix some pleasure with our business."

Along with the martial arts, had he picked up a little mystic mind reading? Or was her attraction to him that obvious? "Tempting though the offer is," she replied honestly, "I discovered my friend hadn't left after all." She made a pretense of looking around. "I'll have to go and find him."

"Oh." His expression was sincerely disappointed. "Need any help?"

"No, that's all right. I'll ring your hotel in the morning," Jessie assured him, starting to walk away.

Simon watched the luscious sway of her hips,

feeling a stirring within himself. "Afraid he'll be jealous?"

She looked at him curiously. "It's not like that. We're just friends," she found herself explaining though she had no idea why.

"I'm glad," Simon said softly. "Good night."

"Good night." Jessie walked away quickly, not trusting herself or the odd, warm sensation she felt deep within her. For many other reasons than his physical training, Simon Taylor was a very dangerous man.

Polished steel and shining, hand-lacquered hardwood gleamed at her from the table as she stepped into Simon's room the next morning. Here was a sampling of his collection, old and valuable, treasured by Simon more for the history and honor they represented than their worth on the market.

Simon had sounded strange when she had phoned earlier, distracted and vague. Face to face, Jessie could once again feel the tension in him, see the mixture of confusion and purpose in his eyes. All was not right, and she knew without question it had something to do with the notebook.

"Are you all right?" she asked.

"What? Oh, I'm fine," Simon answered. He was frowning, and Jessie could tell his mind was far away from her and this supposed business meeting. "Just tired. The day after a match is always the worst."

"May I?" Jessie indicated the weaponry on the table.

"Be my guest."

Another knock sounded on the hotel room door, and Simon went to answer it while Jessie looked over his collection. He came back pushing a room service cart.

"These pieces are lovely," Jessie remarked. "If they're any indication of the quality of the rest of your collection, I can see why you're so choosy about new acquisitions."

Simon looked at her intently, more aware of her presence now than earlier. She looked lovely, fresh and full of life in a vibrant red shirt-waist dress. The style suited her, but then he found it hard to picture any style that wouldn't. He wished things were different, that they really were just strangers who had met and that he could linger on in New York and get to know her better. But that was now quite impossible.

"Do you think I'd be interested in seeing the *Katana* you have for sale?" he asked.

Jessie turned back to the finely crafted blades, marveling at the way sunlight brought patterns alive in the tempered steel. Now that she knew the depth of his expertise, carrying this charade much further would be tricky. It had been a ruse to get closer to him, and it had worked, but from there on she would have to stall.

"I believe so," she said with deliberate hesitation. "I'll get in touch with the other party and see if I can arrange to show it to you."

Simon seemed pleased. "Good." He waved a hand at the breakfast cart. "Now, shall we eat?"

"Let's. That coffee smells wonderful," Jessie replied, taking the seat he offered her.

The food was up to Plaza standards—excellent eggs Benedict, fruit salad, and pastry. They enjoyed every morsel. Simon sipped his coffee and looked at Jessie, trying to decide if he should tell her about his imminent departure. Friend or foe, he supposed she would find out soon enough anyway.

"When I asked you to breakfast last night, I had thought we could make a day of it. I get to Manhattan with some frequency, but never have the time to play tourist," he began.

"Sounds wonderful. I live here and haven't even been to the top of the Empire State building. We could—"

"Unfortunately," Simon continued, "something's come up and I have to leave this morning."

"Oh." Jessie was disappointed. Besides the opportunity to dig for more information, a day with Simon had indeed sounded wonderful. She forced her mind back on track. She had expected him to make some kind of move soon, especially after the unusual turn of events last night—but not this soon. It was desperately important to know where he was going and why.

"Any trouble?"

"Just some . . . family matters," he replied hesitantly. He fixed her with an appraising gaze, judging her reaction. "It seems my brother has gotten himself into some kind of scrape with his employers."

Jessie took a drink of orange juice, carefully keeping her expression neutral. "Nothing serious, I hope."

"I don't really know. I'm just going home to be there if he needs me."

"Is your brother in Dallas?" she asked casually. Two could play at this cat-and-mouse game.

Simon's eyes searched hers. "Dallas?"

"That program from the tournament," she explained, "had a wealth of information about you."

"I see. No, he lives here, but he's been traveling a great deal lately. If he needs a place to rest up he visits me in Texas."

There was a challenge in Simon's voice, a warrior's warning in his eyes. He had evidently accepted her as being a dealer in collectibles, but his continued suspicion was just as evident. He was testing her, drawing the line and daring her to cross over and reveal herself. If she did, she could tell he was fully prepared to defend his brother by whatever means necessary. The thought didn't please her.

"You must be very close," she observed.

"We are." Again the silent threat.

She had to regain his trust, reassure him. The words she chose were easy for her, because they were all true. "I'm sorry we won't get to spend more time together today. Thank you for breakfast, and dinner last night." Putting her hand lightly atop his, she added, "I hope everything turns out all right with your brother."

Simon had marvelous, expressive eyebrows. He raised them in mild surprise. "I'm sure it will." Smiling, he stood up and poured her some more coffee. "Would you mind if I went on with my packing while we talk?"

"When does your flight leave?"

"Eleven o'clock out of La Guardia."

Jessie glanced at her watch. "Oh, my! I think I've taken up enough of your time."

"Not at all. It was very pleasant," he said, losing himself in the depths of her eyes for a moment. "I mean that, Jessie."

She stood up and took his offered hand, trying to ignore the tingle she felt when their skin touched. "It was very nice meeting you too, Simon. Can you give me a number where I can reach you? I've been known to go to great lengths to make a sale."

"All the way to Dallas?"

"Even farther, if necessary," she answered with a grin.

Simon took a card from his wallet and handed it to her. It bore the name of his karate schools and numbers for his office and home.

"I'm looking forward to seeing you again, Jessie."

"The feeling is very mutual, Simon," she replied cheerfully. "As soon as I find out about the sword, I'll be in touch."

Simon escorted her to the door, trying to contain his knowing smile. "I'm sure you will be. Good-bye."

When she had gone, his smile disappeared completely. Just what had Paul gotten him involved in? The odd phone call about papers his brother needed, the notebook with the combination to his own safe in Dallas and another, equally familiar set of numbers. Bits and pieces of information that, in the wrong hands, would be useless. It was a message, now complete, yet one that wouldn't have meant anything to anyone but the two of them.

He knew what he had to do, where he had to go, and it still didn't make a bit of sense. Whatever it was, it was dangerous. At the bottom of the notebook page Paul had written BE CAREFUL in big, bold letters. TRUST NO ONE.

The task was simple enough. Get the papers

and take them to Paul. The trick was not to let anyone else get the papers once he had them and to get them to his brother without being followed. Simon felt quite capable of defending himself and his possessions, but evading somebody determined to follow him was something he'd only seen in the movies or on television.

Perhaps an even more troubling matter was where Jessie McMillan fit into all this. At first he thought she had been sent by Paul, then had decided she was after him. Now a bombshell of new information had him more confused than ever.

He was not without contacts in the world of Japanese collectibles. If a sword of the prestigious nature Jessie had described was available, he would have been among the first to know about it—assuming it was being offered legally, that is.

Though he never dealt in black-market goods, he knew those who did. A few phone calls late last night confirmed there was no such weapon to be had there either. Then came the question he found himself asking without really wanting to know the answer. Did they know of a Jessie McMillan? The name hadn't been familiar, but the description rang a bell. She was a thief, they said, a professional of very high caliber, but had retired.

A collector of sorts, Simon thought as he finished his packing and called for a bellhop. That had been Jessie's description of herself. *Who acquired things here and sold them there.* Was it possible she wasn't trying to sell him a new item for his collection but instead was trying to *steal* his collection?

The more he thought about this startling development, the more uneasy he became. Assuming his information was correct—and he had his doubts, considering the disreputable sources —one question still wracked his brain all the way back to Dallas. *Why now?* Why had she shown up at the precise time Paul had gotten in trouble? Perhaps it was a coincidence, but Simon didn't believe it for a moment. He really was looking forward to seeing Jessie again, because she had a lot of questions to answer.

CHAPTER FOUR

Miles watched forlornly as Jessie joined the line of passengers waiting to board the three-ten flight to Dallas. She looked especially lovely that day, dressed in a crisp tan cotton skirt and matching jacket. Her pink blouse emphasized the bloom of color on her cheeks, put there by the excitement of being on a case.

Miles knew she was right in saying he wasn't her type. The only relationship they would ever have was the one they had shared for so long; they were friends, confidants. He played the role of trusted business contact, teacher and advisor, she was the little sister.

What was more, he liked their relationship. The fact that his romantic life wasn't going anywhere at the moment didn't give him the right to blame her. But he had known her for a long time, and that *did* give him the right to worry about her.

"I wish you wouldn't do this," he said.

With his shaggy black hair, dark expressive eyes, and bushy brows, Miles cut a striking if rather unusual figure, especially in his impeccably tailored blue suit. In reality a very gentle man, he had the veneer of a suave and sophisticated man of the world who had seen it all and been a participant more often than a spectator.

"I was hired to find Paul Taylor," Jessie explained for what seemed the fifteenth time. "And Simon is the only link I have at the moment. I have to keep on his tail."

"I mean I wish you wouldn't do *any* of this." Miles scowled at her. "What kind of occupation is this for—"

"For a woman?" Jessie completed.

"For *anyone!*" he shot back irritably. Aware of curious glances in his direction, he continued less forcefully. "I just don't understand your preoccupation with danger."

Jessie laughed, her expression one of playful reproach. "Don't you lecture me about risk taking, Miles Delaney. Not with your background."

The hustle and bustle of the airport added to her excitement. Combined with thoughts of following Simon and perhaps catching his brother, Jessie was indeed riding an adrenaline high.

"But I quit that life," Miles countered her accusation.

"Because your knees wouldn't take you up the side of one more building, and because that cop said he'd be looking for your signature on every safecracking job he investigated from then on."

"Ssh!" Miles looked around warily. "Okay, so my brilliant career was cut short by bad joints and a recognizable style," he said quietly. "Can I help it if I have so much pride in my crafts that I autograph any safe I touch?"

"Poor Miles," Jessie sympathized. "Doomed to be a gentleman gambler. How much did you make last year?"

Miles grinned sheepishly for a moment, then his frown returned. "Stop changing the subject. We were discussing your risky way of making money, not mine. I may know some potentially dangerous characters, but *you* insist on following them around."

"And *you* are the one who got me interested in this line of work. When you turned state's evidence in that insurance scam caper, *I* was the one who did the digging for you," she pointed out. "Remember?" she asked tauntingly.

Miles shrugged, knowing she was right but not willing to give in. "It was only right. You were my apprentice, after all."

"A fact that didn't escape the attention of that detective either," Jessie said, shaking her finger at him. "We *both* had to find other occupations. We may get into some dangerous situations together on occasion, but at least now we're on the right side of the law."

"I suppose you're right," he admitted grumpily.

"We're not so different, you know," she pointed out. "You take calculated risks, so do I. And Simon Taylor isn't dangerous." At least not in the sense Miles meant. "This job is a piece of cake. I'm good at what I do and I'm well paid for it. What's more, I enjoy the work. What else is there to life, Miles dear?"

Jessie was well aware that part of the excitement she felt was from the mere thought of seeing Simon again. Playing cat and mouse with a man she was attracted to had its dangers, but she had no choice. She had to play the odds and not let her fascination with Simon get in the way.

Miles seemed well aware of what she was thinking. "All right. Just make sure you take care of business instead of the business taking care of you. In the midst of all that enjoyment you might find yourself getting hurt." He sighed in resignation and fixed her with a worried gaze. "I'm sounding like a mother hen. End of lecture."

Jessie handed her ticket to the man at the boarding ramp, then turned to look at Miles with mild surprise. "Why, Miles," she said airily, "I think you're more concerned for my heart than you are for my hide. I'm just following one man to find another man. What's all this about getting hurt?"

Lifting one dark brow, he kissed her quickly on the cheek. "We've known each other for a long time, Jessie. I kid you about it a lot, but I know there's not as much steel in you as you like everyone to think."

This conversation was making her uncomfortable. "I'll be in touch. Keep your ear to the network for me."

"I will." He glanced at his watch. "I'm hopping a flight to Vegas in another hour. You know where to reach me."

Jessie grabbed the opportunity to lighten his mood. "What would Caesars Palace do without you?"

"Crumble to the ground, I imagine." He smiled. "See you soon. Take care."

"I will," she assured him, then strode down the ramp to the waiting plane, trying to ignore a little gnawing feeling of doubt. What awaited her in Dallas? Simon certainly, his brother maybe. Another job, nothing more. Why did she keep getting visions of a certain pair of soulful brown eyes?

Located in a posh suburb of Dallas, Simon's house was a rambling multilevel brick home with a well-tended lawn. A wall, also brick, surrounded the property, combining with a great number of spreading oak and pecan trees to give the place a secluded quality. The sun was vicious even in October, but with a patience born of long practice, Jessie settled down to a boring afternoon of watching Simon relax beside his azure backyard pool. If only they could change places.

She sat in her rental car, sipping iced tea and munching the sandwich she had grabbed at a nearby convenience store. Cursing the humidity that caused even her thin blouse and jeans to feel like too much clothing, she divided her attention between her tasteless lunch and Simon's house.

After arriving in Dallas yesterday, she had settled into a hotel room and rented the car, then tried to set up a surveillance post across the street from Simon's house where the shade would be better. She had learned to pick a spot and stick with it; people noticed a new car in the neighborhood on the first day, then the second day one simply became a part of the scenery. Unfortunately, the brick wall had effectively blocked all view of Simon's home, and with darkness closing in she had called it quits until early this morning.

So there she sat, patient but uncomfortable, watching for signs of movement from a vantage point on a higher street behind the attractive house. Using binoculars, she could see Simon sitting at a poolside table, shaded by a gaily colored umbrella. He was wearing dark-blue swim trunks, his hair still damp from the swim she had so longingly watched him take moments earlier.

Aside from the heat, watching Simon was hardly an unpleasant task. She enjoyed the way his sleek, tanned body sliced through the water when he swam, was mesmerized by the interplay of muscles along his back and thighs when he climbed out of the pool. Even in repose, sitting reading a magazine, Jessie could see a tautness to his masculine form that spoke of great power and agility.

She tried to stop them, but thoughts of what his skin would feel like against hers kept springing into her mind, making the day seem even hotter than it was. Heat waves shimmered in the air, encouraging a dreamlike quality, and she began to think of Simon in a less than professional manner. There was a tension in her too, and not all of it came from sitting and waiting.

A telephone sat on the table beside him, and she saw him pick it up occasionally, imagining the deep, confident tones of his voice and watching his lips move, in her mind's eye seeing them come closer to hers, touching, the taste of his tongue, his breath soft on her cheek. Then a trickle of perspiration would run down between her breasts, waking her from her sensuous daydreams.

By the time evening was closing in, Jessie felt certain she would be insane by that time tomorrow. She had staked out men before—suspected embezzlers, the occasional cheating spouse, one quite handsome business executive under suspicion of industrial espionage. But none had ever affected her this way. She had to see Simon up close, talk to him again.

It was against her normal procedure to leave her post for more than a few minutes. Whatever was going to happen might very well take place under cover of darkness. But what if he had been telling the truth? What if he was waiting too, had simply returned home to be there should Paul need him? She wasn't going to sweat through another day like this with such a possibility hanging over her head. It was time for a more direct approach.

Back at her hotel room, after a cool, invigorating shower, Jessie took Simon's business card from her purse and dialed the home phone number printed there.

"Hello?"

"Simon? This is Jessie. Jessie McMillan."

There was a pause. Jessie could practically see him collecting his thoughts. She could almost see his puzzled, wary expression. His voice sent a tingle down her spine that made her wary too, albeit for an entirely different reason.

"Hello there, Jessie," Simon replied at last. His voice was indeed cautious, but she thought she could detect a certain amount of pleasure in his tone as well. "This doesn't sound like long distance."

"It isn't. I'm here, in Dallas. I'm afraid I have some bad news."

"Oh? And what might that be?" he asked cautiously.

Jessie smiled to herself, her eyes twinkling with mischief. "The party with the sword has decided not to sell. I'm sorry for getting your hopes up. No hard feelings?"

"Not at all." There was another pause. When he spoke again there was even more suspicion in his voice, just as Jessie had expected there would be.

"You've come a long way just to save the price of a long-distance phone call," Simon added.

Jessie laughed, trying to ease the tension. "I only have to fly another six hundred miles this month and they'll give me a toaster." She heard Simon chuckling and continued, "Seriously, I needed a vacation from the city and Dallas sounded nice."

"Dallas is a city too, Jessie."

"But so much slower paced. I like it here." She

suppressed a sarcastic laugh. "I spent the day in the sun."

"Be careful," Simon warned with more than a trace of seriousness. "You might get burned."

"I'll be careful." Jessie sat down on the bed, finding it not at all difficult to put a playfully sensuous edge to her voice. *Must be the torrid climate*, she decided. "Actually, I thought I might get a peek at the rest of your collection if I came down here, as well as cash in a raincheck for a day of sightseeing."

"How about a night of sightseeing instead?"

The question took her so by surprise that Jessie found herself agreeing without thinking about the possible consequences. "Sounds lovely." But just what sights did he have in mind? "Dallas night life?" she asked quickly.

"Sort of," Simon hedged. "If you can be ready in half an hour, I'll take you to the fair."

"Fair?"

"The Texas State Fair, of course. Some of my students are giving a demonstration there this evening, but after that we can wander around and pretend we're innocent tourists."

"All right." Jessie told him where she was and hung up, wondering what he had meant. *Pretend we're innocent tourists?* Evidently his suspicions about her were still alive and well, but she didn't care.

She already knew he was very intelligent.

Perhaps he knew exactly what she wanted and had decided to wait her out until she made the first move. If so, it had worked, and again she didn't care. One more day of sweltering surveillance would've had her bouncing off the walls. If he confronted her that evening, perhaps she would end the charade and tell him the whole story. Paul Taylor would be much better off in her hands than in those of the people he had double-crossed. The tricky part would be convincing Simon of that fact.

When he picked her up at her hotel a half hour later, however, everything seemed back to normal. Jessie decided that either she had imagined the suspicion in his voice or Simon was a better actor than she gave him credit for.

"I really am sorry we won't be able to do business," she told him on the ride to the fairgrounds. "Evidently the man with the sword decided he couldn't part with it."

"Understandable," Simon replied. He glanced at her, somewhat disturbed at just how happy he was to see her again. "A *Katana* like that is a real treasure. I'm surprised he put it on the market in the first place."

"Well, it wasn't really ever *on* the market, exactly. Wishful thinking on my part, I guess."

Simon considered her explanation as he pulled past the guard at the entrance to the fair parking lot. If the illusive sword she spoke of was never really for sale, that would explain why neither he nor any of his sources had heard about it. As for the other information he'd obtained about Jessie, he couldn't believe it. She just didn't look like a thief. Right now, in form-fitting designer jeans and a billowy turquoise blouse, she looked like a vision of loveliness, not a burglar.

Still, her showing up abruptly, both in New York and there, was more coincidence than he could easily accept. Time would tell, and he could think of worse ways to spend the time before he made his move than escorting Jessie around Dallas.

"The place is packed this evening," he observed, searching for a parking spot among the rows reserved for employees and participants. "Ah, here we are." He parked the car, then led the way across the immense expanse of fairgrounds to a raised platform amid a noisy throng of people.

Leaving Jessie to watch a group of square dancers, Simon went to give last-minute encouragement to his karate students waiting on the sidelines. He disappeared for a while, then came back dressed in a karate uniform, stiff white with the honored black belt around his waist.

Jessie enjoyed their demonstration, as did the crowd around her, taking special delight in watching Simon and his students break boards and bricks with various parts of their bodies. Afterward, Simon and his crew circulated among the people and talked about their school, giving out pamphlets and gift certificates for free lessons.

"Get any new recruits?" she asked when Simon returned to her side.

"A few, maybe. Once they find out there's more sweat involved than flashy movements, most lose interest," he explained goodnaturedly. "You can never tell, though. Besides, my students really enjoy putting on these shows. They consider it an honor to be selected."

After Simon changed, they strolled down the midway, ignoring the taunting cries of hawkers from the sharpshooting and dart-throwing booths. People jostled them from all sides, infecting them with their excitement.

"I really enjoyed that one student, the young girl with the brown belt."

"Amanda?" Simon chuckled. "She's a tiger. I pity the poor boy who tries to force *her* into a good-night kiss."

"Or the poor boy who doesn't offer when she wants him to," Jessie added.

It was the largest fair Jessie had ever attended. Buildings housing all kinds of temporary exhibits were scattered everywhere, as well as the permanent residents of Fair Park, such as an aquarium, a natural history museum, and the hall of Texas history. Jessie especially enjoyed the exhibit of new cars that filled a massive building and spilled out the side doors beneath red-and-white striped awnings.

Enjoyed it, that is, until the models hired as window dressing for the shining automobiles started showing more than casual interest in Simon. A sudden and disturbing feeling of possessiveness gripped Jessie, and she linked her arm defiantly through Simon's.

"I'm hungry," she declared, casually steering him out of the crowded hall.

Grinning in amusement, Simon agreed. "Me too. Shall we eat here, or have you had enough fair?"

"Enough, I think, to last me quite a while," she replied, stopping for a moment to slip off her sandals. The concrete was still hot from baking under the sun all day and felt wonderful on her sore feet. "I should have brought the tennis shoes I wear in Manhattan."

"I always thought that looked so odd," Simon remarked, enjoying the feel of her body next to his as they walked to the car. "Women, dressed in conservative business suits, looking so professional, and wearing those scruffy white tennis shoes."

"You try walking eight blocks in high heels some time, buster, and you wouldn't think it looked odd at all."

71

Simon took them to a cool, casual restaurant nearby where they had a traditional Texas meal of beer and barbecue. So far they had been chatting about the things they saw at the fair, the fish at the aquarium or the flowers in the botanical gardens.

Now, however, the unusual circumstances surrounding their relationship seemed to hit them both at once, and they found themselves looking at each other quietly.

Jessie felt unexplainably shy, tried to fight the feeling by getting back to business. "Sore toes aside, I really had fun. I hope my showing up like this isn't an imposition."

"Imposition?" Simon asked curiously.

"The family business you spoke of in New York. Am I interrupting you getting together with your brother?"

"No," he replied. But she was, in a way. He had decided to bide his time, at least for a little while, until he felt certain he wouldn't be followed when he went to meet Paul. The only evidence of anyone trailing him sat across the table from him now, in the person of this beautiful and mysterious woman.

He wanted to ask her straight out if she was after his brother but something prevented him. He was afraid of what the answer might be. She was looking at him curiously, so he added,

"You're not an imposition at all. I enjoy your company, Jessie."

He fervently hoped she was just what she said she was, a rather unorthodox dealer of collectibles. Any other reason for her presence there would make a deeper relationship with her impossible, and he wanted more than anything to get to know Jessie better—much better.

The soft honesty in Simon's voice was melting Jessie's businesslike attitude. Then again, whom was she trying to fool? As far as Simon was concerned, her supposed business with him was at an end. But once he knew her true purpose, she doubted he would want to see her again. Should she tell him what she hoped to find in Dallas— his brother—or admit to herself she was enjoying his company too much to reveal her charade?

"Simon, I—"

"Now," Simon interrupted, almost afraid of what she might be about to say, "I think we should fulfill that curiosity of yours concerning my collection, don't you?"

Jessie smiled, glad the moment of decision was past. "Why not?" she answered. She told herself it would be a good opportunity to snoop around for traces of Paul Taylor, but deep down she knew she was rationalizing. She wanted to go. "You don't by any chance have a pool?"

"Doesn't everyone?" Simon replied haughtily.

"I'd love a swim. We could stop by my hotel and I'll grab my suit."

"That won't be necessary."

The gleam in his eyes gave her pause. "Um . . ."

"I think there's a suit at the house that will fit you."

"Oh. A forgetful lady friend?"

Did he imagine it, or did those eyes of hers suddenly get a bit greener? "No, a very moral-minded housekeeper. The thought of someone being forced to skinny dip for the lack of a suit made her go out and buy a few spares," he explained as he led her out of the restaurant.

Simon's house was just as well kept and attractive inside as out, and his collection of Japanese military hardware was nothing short of spectacular. Though impressed with the museum-quality collection, Jessie's mind was mainly on the inviting waters of Simon's swimming pool.

For his part, Simon was confused. He didn't know whether to be comforted or alarmed by her polite but obviously distracted attention as she examined his collection. If Jessie was a thief, wouldn't she take more interest in the individual pieces he showed her, and especially in the security arrangements? He finally decided to stop being paranoid and simply enjoy her company.

"The spare suits are in that closet," he told her when they had finished their tour of the house. "I'll be waiting for you by the pool." He closed the door to the guest bedroom on his way out and went to change, grinning with anticipation.

"I think you lied to me," Jessie accused him when she emerged from the house a bit later. The pool area was softly illuminated, and the pool itself was lighted and very inviting. She clutched the towel she had wrapped around her as she tested the water with her foot.

Simon, already in the water, looked admiringly at her long, shapely legs. "About what?"

"No moral-minded housekeeper would have chosen this suit." Deciding she was being overly modest, Jessie removed her towel and put it on a chair. After all, she had gotten herself into this, had no one to blame for this sensuous moonlight swim but herself. And she was proud of her body; heaven knew she worked hard enough to keep trim and fit.

"Hmm." Simon hummed in appreciation. "I see what you mean. A salesclerk must have pulled a fast one on her."

There was no mistaking the pleasure and desire in his eyes as Simon watched her slide gracefully into the water beside him. The bikini was daringly cut, displaying Jessie's lush cleavage and firm, athletic thighs. Her stomach was softly rounded and feminine, her hips full yet trim and decidedly inviting. It was all he could do to keep from pulling her to him instantly.

"I assure you," Jessie said, reveling in the feel of the cool water surrounding her, "my own suit is much more conservative."

"In that case, I'll have to remember to give my housekeeper a raise."

She splashed him and took off across the pool with sure, confident strokes, hoping that activity would relieve some of the tension she felt building within her. This had seemed like a good idea at the time, but now she was wondering if she hadn't made a serious error. She could sense the desire Simon felt for her, knew it to be matched by her own. Those muscular thighs, his broad back and powerful arms. The brief, tight cut of his suit wasn't lost on her either. She swam faster.

Simon pulled up beside her and matched her pace, easily keeping up with her, enjoying the view of her nicely shaped derriere as she turned and pushed off the edge of the pool.

"Having a good time?" he asked when they had completed several lengths.

Jessie stopped, slightly winded by her exertions. Simon was grinning from ear to ear. Obviously she wasn't going to wear him out.

"Yes, thanks," she said, puffing.

"Me too." His eyebrows bobbed up and down, and he gazed appraisingly at her scantily clad form, silhouetted by the pool lights through the crystal-clear water. "You're in very good shape."

She knew he didn't just mean her swimming ability. A slight chill shook her even though the night air was quite warm. "So are you." She could hardly ignore the well-defined muscles of his chest and stomach, the effortless movement of his arms and legs as he kept himself afloat.

Suddenly feeling a bit dizzy, Jessie grabbed for the pool edge, missed, slipped below the water momentarily, and came up sputtering. Simon grabbed her and pulled her close, keeping them both up with strong kicks of his legs.

"Don't drown, mystery woman," he said softly, his lips touching her ear. "We're just getting to know each other."

The movement of his body against hers felt magical, like every daydream she'd ever had all rolled into one. "M-mystery woman?" she asked, startled by her breathlessness.

Simon lifted her up and sat her on the pool's edge, her legs dangling in the water on either side of him. He looked up into her eyes, his hands gently caressing her calves, then her knees, delighting in her shivering response to his touch.

"Mystery woman. But I'll know all your secrets soon, sweet Jessie," he promised. His fingers traced a lingering path along the sensitive skin of her inner thighs. "Won't I?"

Jessie gasped as his arms went around her waist and he pulled himself closer, rising half out of the water to gently kiss her stomach. "No! Simon, I—"

He released her and pulled himself up to sit beside her, taking possession of her lips with his open mouth. Their tongues touched and Jessie felt the world spin, a warmth creeping outward from the center of her being. Her arms went tentatively around him and he crushed her against his chest, her nipples hard through the thin material of her suit.

This was insane! She was a mystery all right, with a secret that would make him release her like a hot potato should she reveal it. She didn't want to tell him, wanted his caresses to go on and on, but neither could she allow this passion to continue to its inevitable conclusion. She wanted Simon, but she liked him too, and would not lie just to have him.

"Simon, we can't," she whispered hoarsely when she had managed to draw away from him. "There's something you have to know."

The phone on the poolside table rang, an abrupt, jarring, imperious sound. Simon kissed her throat, nipped her gently with his teeth. "Damn," he murmured. "I have to answer that.

It might be . . . I'm expecting an important call."

Then he was on his feet, going to the phone, his smoldering gaze still on Jessie as he answered. "Hello?"

Jessie was torn. What she wanted to do was run, grab her clothes, and leave before the evening ended in heedless passion. But what if that was Paul on the phone? She should stay, find out what was going on, continue to live her lie.

She couldn't. She was a professional, but she was also a woman, and going to bed with a man to gain information was wrong, completely despicable—no matter how much she wanted and desired him. She didn't even want to stay and eavesdrop on his conversation. In view of what had just happened between them, even that seemed too cold-blooded. Perhaps Miles had been right; there just wasn't enough steel in her.

Jessie jumped up and ran back into the house, catching a glimpse of Simon's startled expression as she passed him.

"Hey! Where are you going?" he called after her.

Heedless of his question, she went to the bedroom and hurriedly stripped off her suit, hoping to dress before Simon got off the phone. But she had barely tossed the wet garment aside before he burst through the bedroom door. Clutching a towel around her, Jessie met his questioning gaze, feeling herself grow warm from the hunger she saw in his eyes.

"Mind if I join you?" Simon asked softly. He hooked his thumbs into the waistband of his suit.

Mesmerized, Jessie still managed to utter a weak protest. "S-Stop!"

"Stop? Oh, I see." He stepped over to her, his eyes gleaming in the darkened room, reflecting the moonlight streaming through the window. "Would you rather undress me yourself?"

"No! We can't . . ."

Jessie's hands felt weak, no match for the strength of Simon's as he unwrapped his prize, revealing her damp, tempting body to his view. He pulled her against him, a deep moan of masculine pleasure his response to the feel of her breasts pressing on his chest.

"Jessie. You feel so good," Simon murmured. He took possession of her mouth once more, his tongue plunging between her lips, an erotic, sensuous invasion.

He felt good, too, the heated skin of his hard male form touching her breasts, her stomach, her thighs. Jessie's mind swam, realizing she was lost, her hands wandering of their own volition around his sides to his back, reveling in the taut muscles beneath her fingertips. All the logical arguments, every one of the reasons why she shouldn't make love to Simon, were as dust in the wind. Her professionalism was no match for the desire she felt leap within her as he dipped his head to nip lightly at the skin of her neck.

"I want you, sweet Jessie."

His voice, demanding yet gentle, seemed to dance along her nerve endings, making her shiver with delight. She wanted him, too, more than she had wanted any man before. The strength of her passion scared her, but even that ceased to matter when he lifted her into his arms and carried her to his bed.

The sheets were cool on her skin, a chill that was quickly chased away by her thoughts as Simon removed his brief suit and joined her. He was virile and potent, a throbbing masculine presence beside her. She couldn't escape him, and in the last few moments of coherent thought left to her, she realized she didn't want to. He didn't really know her, so in a sense she was living a lie. But this wasn't a lie, not the feel of his body next to hers, the touch of his hands and taste of his lips. Her need, her desire for him, wasn't a lie either. This was real, a passion she couldn't control.

"I want you too, Simon," Jessie managed to say breathlessly. Then his deft touch brought an end to the need for words.

Nor could Simon speak, stunned into silence by her beauty and lithe responsiveness. Her hands upon him, feather-light yet bold, drove him to a wild abandon he hadn't known possible. Their desire consumed them as they stroked each other, and soon mere touch alone was not enough. Simon sought the center of her being, moving slowly yet relentlessly until their bodies fit together in fiery union.

Jessie cried out in mindless joy, her fingers kneading the solid flesh and muscle of his buttocks as Simon worked his potent magic. Deep within her, trapped by her silky femininity, the tension of a desire too long denied made his every muscle taut. Jessie moaned in sympathy and delight, for every sinew of her body felt stretched with the same tension. They strove together for release, tumbling into the abyss and shuddering in passionate delight.

Breathless, they lay in a damp tangle, cuddled close and bathing in the afterglow. Less urgent now, Simon's caresses lulled her into a soft, pleasant sleep. She dozed, feeling the comforting movement of his own gradually deepening breathing.

Jessie awoke with a start, an overwhelming feeling of guilt flooding into her consciousness. What had she done? Then she looked at Simon's peaceful face, tenderness replacing her alarm. How could she berate herself for what had just happened? She could no more have stopped the desire between them from reaching this inevitable conclusion than she could stop her own heart from beating.

But she had to get out of here before one moment of abandon became something more. Her guard had slipped, as she had known all along it probably would. She had gotten carried away, couldn't blame herself for being human. Simon, however, might view things differently.

Jessie suddenly felt panicked and confused. How could she tell him the whole story now? Considering the lies and half-truths she had already told, it was possible he would see the ecstasy they had shared as just another ruse on her part—though nothing could be further from the truth. She had wanted him, still wanted him, found herself wishing they had indeed just been strangers who happened to meet. But they weren't. She had a job to do, and even though she couldn't have stopped it, by making love to Simon she had just complicated things beyond belief.

Careful not to wake him, she extricated herself from his warm embrace and hurriedly started to put on her clothes. She had to get out of here before he woke up, think through this insane situation.

But he wasn't as deeply asleep as she had thought. His eyes opened, and he frowned. Getting out of bed and putting on his robe, he watched her, puzzled by her actions.

"What are you doing?" he demanded.

"It's getting late," Jessie replied, fumbling

with the buttons on her blouse. "I really should be going."

"I'd hardly call eleven-thirty late." Simon stepped over to her, taking her hands in his. "Especially to a big city girl. Besides," he added softly, kissing her fingertips, "I thought we were going to trade secrets."

Jessie's mind told her to make a full confession, but her body reminded her that if she did, and he decided she had simply been using him, she might never again feel the excitement of Simon's touch. She was too confused, too deep within his spell, to make a rational decision.

"I have to go."

Simon had other ideas. He pulled her into his arms again, once more tasting the sweetness of her honeyed mouth. "Where?" he murmured. "What could possibly be more important than this?" His lips blazed a trail of fire across her cheek, down her delicate neck to the swelling softness of the tops of her barely concealed breasts.

Jessie shuddered, almost giving in to the temptation of his seduction. He was gently pushing her toward the bed behind them. In a moment neither of them would be doing any talking, so she had better do some now—and fast.

"I—I thought southern men were slow and

cautious," she managed to say, trying to hold her ground.

"I'm not a southerner, I'm a Coloradan. When we see something we want, we go after it," Simon whispered in her ear. "Again and again."

Jessie pushed against his chest. "And I'm a New Yorker. When we see something coming at us this fast, we get out of the way." And she did just that, stepping aside and twisting from his grasp. Momentarily off balance, Simon sprawled unceremoniously onto the bed.

He looked up at her and grinned. "Circular movement to avoid an attacker," he said with surprised admiration. "I thought you said you weren't a student of the martial arts."

"I'm not," she replied, struggling to regain control over her breathing. "That's a basic survival technique when hailing a taxi."

To her astonishment—and great relief—Simon wasn't angry and didn't renew his sensuous assault. He roared with laughter. Still, Jessie watched him warily as he rolled off the bed and got to his feet.

"You'll have to come down to the school as a guest instructor," he said at last, still chuckling.

Hands on her hips, Jessie regarded him suspiciously. "What would you call the course? Street smarts?"

"How about bedroom tactics?"

"You're outrageous!" She laughed with him

despite the tumult of emotions still racing through her.

Their eyes met, and for a moment Jessie feared the battle would begin again. Then Simon approached her slowly, and put his hands on her shoulders. "You're too much woman to ignore, Jessie. And I'm not about to apologize for what just happened between us."

"Simon—"

He put a finger on her lips to silence her. "Solve at least one mystery for me. You were about to leave before I swept you off your feet," he said with a wry grin. "And you're about to leave now. Why?"

"It's just that there are so many things you don't know about me," she said hesitantly.

"Then tell me. Please?"

His eyes were so warm upon her that she almost did. But something held her back. Maybe it was her fear that doing so would end any chance for their relationship. Maybe it was the surge of professionalism telling her she had a job to do and her feelings for him would have to wait.

Jessie sighed and turned away, unable to look at him. "I can't. It's all so complicated." *That* was a major understatement. If she tried to convince him of her good intentions now and failed, she might lose the best chance she had of locating Paul. If she didn't try, she might lose Simon.

Simon stood there, frowning, wondering why

she wasn't looking at him, and why she was being so secretive. All the suspicions he had lost sight of in the last few hours came flooding back. As warm, passionate, and willing as she had been in his arms, the questions she refused to answer worried him. Jessie could be a thief, or a spy from the investment firm, or even an angry investor bent on revenge. Whatever she was, her sudden appearance in his life was not the pleasant coincidence he had hoped.

"I see." He glared at her. "You'll share my bed, but you won't share your secrets."

His words hurt her deeply. How could he possibly think she had just jumped into bed with him on a lark? "I don't think it's any secret how much I like you, Simon," Jessie said quietly. "Or how attracted I am to you. Not now, not after . . ."

"Then tell me what's going on," he demanded.

Try as she might, the explanation he was looking for simply stuck in her throat. "I can't."

"In that case, I think you're right," he said, his tone now full of quiet threat. "It is time for you to leave."

There was no mistaking the finality in his voice, the sour note of betrayal. He may not know exactly what she was after, but he would have his suspicions. A new sense of purpose filled her. In a week or two, or however long it took to find his brother, Simon would know the truth. Then the fact that she had been trying to help Paul and not hurt him would be apparent —she hoped. Only after this was all over could she be honest and explore the wonderful feelings Simon had awakened in her tonight.

"I'll call you a cab," Simon said perfunctorily on his way out the door.

Jessie took a moment and collected her thoughts, forcing her emotions back into a hiding spot deep inside. When she emerged from the bedroom, she had finally regained her protective veil of detachment. Her mind was once again functioning on the cool level that had won her a reputation as a competent professional.

"The cab is on the way. I'm sure you can find your way out," Simon said flatly.

"Thank you. And Simon?"

"Yes?"

"I want you to know how much I enjoyed this evening. I meant what I said. I like you very much."

"I like you too, Jessie McMillan, but I'll be damned if I know why." He frowned, hesitated a moment, then shrugged and went outside to sit in the shadows by the pool.

CHAPTER FIVE

Dawn found Jessie back at her post outside Simon's home, once again a frustrated observer and cursing her own impetuous behavior of last night. She hadn't gotten much sleep, pacing her hotel room like a caged tigress until she had finally accepted the truth. By allowing her attraction to Simon to cloud her thinking, she'd blown her chances of getting the information she needed.

Now all she could do was wait and watch. He had asked her to leave and undoubtedly he wouldn't talk to her unless she was prepared to explain herself. If she tried that and failed to convince him of her good intentions, he might become even more cautious than he already was.

That would only delay the inevitable. She would find his brother, but she wanted it to be sooner, not later. She wanted to get all this behind them, prove herself in Simon's eyes, feel his arms around her once again.

A light, misty rain fell for most of the morning, then burned off around noon, making the day terribly muggy as the damp ground gave up its moisture under the hot sun. Jessie felt like she was in a steam bath. Her lack of sleep caught up with her during the long, boring afternoon, and she nodded off, waking with a start to a cool breeze and impending nightfall.

She yawned and stretched, chiding herself for the lapse in her surveillance but glad for the rest. She now felt bright-eyed and alert. The coffee she'd brought in a Thermos was lukewarm, but she drank it anyway as she watched the lights come on one by one in Simon's house. Suddenly she made a mad grab for her binoculars, her pulse quickening with a surge of adrenaline.

A car was purring slowly up Simon's street, the driver apparently looking for something—or someone. She crouched down instinctively, her eyes widening as the car pulled into Simon's driveway.

"What have we here?" she murmured softly to herself.

It was hard to tell in the gathering darkness, but she was fairly certain it was a man who got out of the car and was welcomed inside Simon's home immediately. She waited as long as she could, peering through her binoculars and trying to get a glimpse of Simon and his visitor. The shadows of night finally closed in around her. She fidgeted uncertainly for a while, then decided to go in for a closer look.

Clouds drifted across the sky, obscuring the weak light of a quarter moon as Jessie climbed out of her car. She opened the trunk, spent a few minutes preparing for the sneaky task ahead, then glided silently down the street toward the rear of Simon's house.

A stocky, well-dressed man sat on Simon's couch, dividing his attention between the martini he held in his hand and his obviously distracted client. His manner of speaking was fast and direct, yet full of encouragement.

"Enrollment's up fifty percent over last year, you'll be opening another *dojo* in Arlington later this month, and your stock portfolio is so healthy your broker is thinking about starting his own newsletter." The man took another gulp of his drink and glared at Simon. "So would you mind telling me why you're so blasted uptight?"

Simon glared back. He was standing in the middle of the living room, his fists clenched at his sides, angry at the whole world. Paul was in trouble, he had thrown the most desirable woman he'd ever met out of his house last night, and now his business manager was on his case for taking a few days off.

"Barney," he managed to say through clenched teeth, "I told you I needed a rest last month and the month before that. What do you do? You book me for every shopping mall opening and two-bit tournament you can find. And while we're on the subject, that loss in New York is on your head, not mine. I was suffering from jet lag so bad I could barely see the guy I was fighting."

"Now, Simon, I—"

"No," he interrupted. He made a visible effort to calm down before continuing. "No more. This time you're going to listen to me. I am on vacation. I have some family problems to straighten out, and I want to explore a couple of other things that have recently caught my attention."

Like Jessie's involvement in this whole affair, her jade-green eyes, and the lovely sounds she made when he touched her. It was insane, in view of her suspicious behavior, but he had never wanted a woman that much in his life.

"But you're on the comeback trail, boy," Barney objected. "The championship—"

"Will wait. You and I both know these publicity junkets work better after the first of the year anyway. All those people with winter fat looking for some new way to burn it off."

Barney had such a heavy beard it gave even

his clean-shaven face a bluish tint. He ran one hand along his jaw, looking thoughtful, knowing he had lost this argument anyway. He worked for Simon, not the other way around. If his client was adamant about taking some time off, he'd better stop pushing and agree with him.

"Yeah. I could plan a big spring campaign . . ."

At last Simon smiled, taking a seat on the couch with a big sigh. "See? That wasn't so hard, now was it?"

His business manager finished his martini in one final gulp, and shook the couch with his laughter. "Okay. You can't blame me for doing my job, though. I was only trying to look out for your best interests."

Simon slapped him on the back. "And you do it well, Barney. I'm not complaining about the job you've done promoting me and my schools. And I certainly can't complain about the way you're handling the financial end."

He grinned. "We do make a pretty lucrative team."

"Just remember I'm only human."

"Okay, but that's just between you and me. We wouldn't want to ruin your image now, would we?"

He stood up, Simon rising with him, and the two men shook hands. Though it was hard to tell sometimes from the way they argued, they were friends as well as business partners.

"What are you going to do?" Barney asked.

"Oh, I don't know," Simon hedged. Paul's warning echoed in his mind. *Trust no one.* "Maybe I'll take a little trip, do some fishing."

"You said something about family problems?"

"Nothing serious, really. Paul's gotten into a little trouble, that's all," he explained as he escorted Barney to the front door.

Barney raised his eyebrows and chuckled. "Gotten somebody else in trouble, probably." He stepped onto the front porch and gave him a broad wink. "Speaking of which, you should try to find yourself some feminine companionship too. You're so tense it's leaking out of your ears."

"Good night, Barney."

Simon smiled at the irony of his friend's advice. Once this whole mess was taken care of, feminine companionship was exactly what he had in mind. He watched him drive off, then turned on his heel and stopped. Something caught his eye, and he peered into the shadows at the side of the house for a moment. At last he went back inside and closed the door behind him, shaking his head.

"Barney's right," he muttered. "Now I'm starting to see things."

Outside in the darkness, Jessie breathed a sigh of relief. Simon had almost been looking right at her, but her attire made her one with the night. She had on jeans, a black cotton shirt with long sleeves, and her flowing raven hair was piled on top of her head in a chignon. Her pale face looked like a patch of moonlight among the shadows.

Jessie was good at surveillance, though she felt she lacked sufficient patience. She was much better at winding her way into a subject's life, gaining trust, gathering information under the guise of friendly interest. That had been her plan for Simon until she found herself wanting a real friendship with him, allowed her own desires to get in the way of the job she had to do.

Perhaps it was just as well things had developed the way they had. At least this way she wouldn't be faced with lying to Simon anymore. She would now have to operate from the outside, waiting to seize every bit of information that came her way.

Working in the shadows, gliding through the darkness like a wraith. There, in that part of her unusual occupation, she wasn't just fair or good. She was excellent. The need for silence, the fear of being caught, the advance planning required to escape should she be discovered, all heightened her senses to pinpoint sharpness. She felt completely and wonderfully alive.

She also felt disappointed. The stocky man had only been Simon's business manager, Barney. Jessie had caught the end of their conversation using a tiny listening device pressed up against the window. Still, she had gained an interesting snippet of information. Simon had been talking about taking a vacation, perhaps going fishing. It could very well be that instead of Paul coming there, Simon intended to meet his brother somewhere else.

Usually immune to such things, Jessie wondered at the feeling of guilt she had at invading Simon's privacy this way. Evidently whatever spell he had cast on her went much deeper than mere physical attraction. But this was the only option left to her, so she continued to listen, hoping to overhear a phone conversation, maybe a plane reservation being made.

After agonizing minutes of silence the phone did ring. Jessie turned up the volume on her electronic eavesdropper.

"Hello?"

Wishing she could hear the whole conversation, Jessie settled for peering through the window to watch Simon as he spoke. He looked very annoyed at something.

"Not again!" He listened for a moment then shrugged irritably. "Yes, I'll come. But this is the last time, Barney. If you would simply take an occasional look at your gas gauge. . . . Don't give me that. If you couldn't afford to feed it, you would never have bought that gas guzzler

96

in the first place. See you in a couple of minutes."

Jessie watched him hang up the phone, then shrank back into the shadows as he came out the front door muttering under his breath. He got in his car and took off in a hurry.

She crouched beneath the window for a moment, wondering what to do. She needn't worry about following him, but she didn't want to sit there all night either. It occurred to her that this would be a good opportunity to search the house. Maybe she could turn up the notebook Paul had slipped him in New York.

With guilt tugging at her conscience every step of the way, Jessie went around back and stood by the sliding glass doors arguing with herself.

She could get in quite easily there. But she had no idea how long Simon would be gone. On the other hand, she had seen most of the house and figured the notebook would probably be in Simon's study. And yet . . .

Jessie snorted in disgust. *Face it, dear,* she told herself at last. *You like the man too damn much to break into his house and that's all there is to it.* Deciding she'd had enough skulking for one evening, she started her slow, silent way back around the way she had come.

Simon crouched behind the brick wall surrounding his house, hidden in the shadow cast by a giant pecan tree across the street. *If the neighbors see me hiding outside my own house, I'll never be able to show my face at a block party again. Poor Barney would have to fend for himself,* he thought. His legs felt cramped, and the waiting was driving him crazy. What if he was imagining things? His mind pushed away his discomfort and doubt. Someone had been watching him when he left to help Barney, he felt it in his bones.

Finally his waiting paid off. A slender figure flitted across his line of sight, clothed all in black and nearly invisible in the darkness. For a moment the figure disappeared, and he risked a longer peek over the wall, feeling a surge of panic. Burglar or spy, this could be a dangerous encounter, and he couldn't afford to be taken by surprise. Then he heard a soft scrambling sound on the other side of the wall and immediately ducked down again.

Two gloved hands grasped the wall above his head. In a movement that dazed him for a moment, a slim form catapulted over him, landing with an odd metallic thump directly behind his hiding place. He reached out and grabbed the intruder's arm with lightning speed.

"Okay, buddy, I've gotcha," Simon declared.

He held his prize firmly with one hand, the other pulled back in a threatening fist.

Jessie gasped in surprise. "What the—"

"Jessie!" Simon studied her startled face, feeling completely stunned himself. Then his mind began to work again and put the whole scheme together. He spoke with knowing sarcasm. "Just what the hell are you after, lady? As if I didn't know." He kept a firm grip on her arm.

"Just out for my evening constitutional," she replied flippantly. The game was up, and in a way she was relieved. She may as well play it with style. "What are you hiding in the bushes for? Playing cops and robbers?"

"That's really cute, coming from you. And surely a pro can come up with a better lie. The only stroll you were taking was through my collection, and we both know it," he said acidly. "What happened? Forget a bag to carry the booty in?"

Jessie tried not to let her confusion show on her face. What was he talking about? "Simon, I—"

"And don't give me any bull about having second thoughts because of how much I've come to mean to you," he added, his voice rough with sarcasm. "You've been playing me along the whole time, haven't you?"

In the back of her mind a light suddenly dawned. He didn't know she was after his brother, he was accusing her of being a thief. Someone must have leaked information about her, information she had planted in the underground network. Her own cover story had been turned against her. The idea made her angry, but the anger couldn't overcome the hurt his other accusation caused.

Though she had been playing him along in some ways, the feelings she was beginning to have for him were very real. But the only thing she felt like doing now was lashing out at him, to replay him for the pain his words had caused.

"Brilliant deduction," she quipped caustically. "As long as I was casing the joint, I decided I might as well have a little fun with you."

Simon gave her a shake. "We'll see how much fun you have after I've called the cops."

Jessie smiled slightly, satisfied that she had indeed hurt him. It wasn't her imagination; she could see it in his eyes. He had begun to develop feelings for her too. Then her smile faded. She didn't enjoy his pain as much as she thought she would, found herself wanting to apologize and tell him the truth.

Right now, however, getting the heck away from there was the first priority. Sorting out her feelings for this man would have to wait.

"Oh, come on, Simon. Don't be so dramatic," Jessie said, making her voice light and teasing. "You're wise to my plan now. You win. What good will calling the police do?" She thought quickly and added, "Other than complicate both our lives?"

"It would give me one hell of a lot of satisfaction for one thing, Miss McMillan," Simon bit out.

Jessie's heart was pounding like mad. The last thing she wanted was to spend the night in some police station, answering a lot of questions about who she really was and what she was after. And Simon certainly wouldn't have much confidence in her ability to help his brother afterward either.

"So go ahead and call them," she said calmly. In a gesture she hoped would convince him she couldn't care less, she unclipped her hair and shook the raven tresses free. "I'll be back on the streets before you're done filling out the complaint."

Simon had to smile. "You're really something else, Jessie. Cool as ice and beautiful to boot." Besides, she had a point. He couldn't afford to waste time; Paul needed his help and needed it soon. "But what would you do if I let go of you right now?" he asked. "Run away?"

Jessie smiled, her white teeth shining in the darkness. She looked at the hand clamped on her arm. "Now how could I run away from a big strong man like you?"

Simon accepted her challenge without thinking and released her, realizing his mistake too late. In a matter of seconds it all made sense: how he had lost sight of her for a few moments, the metallic thump he'd heard when she'd jumped over the wall. On soft plastic wheels with silent sealed bearings, Jessie glided soundlessly away from him on her roller skates. She was twenty yards from him in a flash.

"Stop!"

"You've got to be kidding!" Jessie called back to him, zipping away with powerful strokes of her legs.

Simon was in very good condition, and fast on his feet, but Jessie had a mechanical advantage and was rapidly disappearing into the darkness ahead of him.

"Damn it, Jessie McMillan, you come back here!"

What good did that do? he asked himself. That might not even be her real name. He stopped running and glared after her. Moments later he heard the sound of a powerful engine growl to life, then fade off into the night.

CHAPTER SIX

Simon sat in his darkened, wood-paneled study, holding some papers in his hand. He had rushed inside after Jessie had gotten away from him, suddenly panicked by the thought that perhaps her target hadn't been his collection after all. But the papers had still been locked securely in his safe, where Paul had put them weeks ago while Simon was out of the country.

The documents outlined the trouble Paul had gotten into, some kind of high-powered stock scheme Simon only vaguely understood. Evidently Paul's supervisor had gotten hold of some illegal inside information on a corporation called Soldyne Technologies. Needing capital to take advantage of the information, he had invited a select group of investors into the deal, the kind of men who liked to make money and didn't ask questions.

Somewhere along the line, however, Paul *had* asked questions, and evidently he hadn't liked the answers. Simon couldn't make heads or tails out of the lists of names, stock transactions, and other information his brother had compiled. But one didn't have to be a genius to see that something shady was going on. And Paul's curiosity had gotten him involved in the whole mess clear up to his neck.

The front money totaled well over a quarter of a million, the profit potential many times that. When Paul developed cold feet and took off, he had crossed someone all right, and crossed him good. Now the only thing that stood between him and a permanent disappearance were these all-important papers.

But at the moment Simon's thoughts were far away from the documents he held and their importance. Right now he had his mind on Jessie. The safe hadn't been touched, his collection was still intact, and she had left nothing behind but questions. Maybe she hadn't had time to steal anything. Maybe she really had developed some kind of feeling for him and couldn't go through with her plans—whatever those plans might be. He could only guess at what her true business was with him.

It really didn't matter, he supposed. He had no intentions of letting her get close enough to do him, his collection, or Paul any harm. At least that's what the logical, rational part of his mind told him. Inside, where he could still see her face and hear her voice, another part of him admitted the undeniable truth. Thief, criminal, spy, or worse, he still found Jessie wonderfully, dangerously attractive. It might end up to be a fatal fascination, but he simply couldn't get her out of his mind.

Despite his inner turmoil, one thing had become clear. Jessie was a rogue element, a danger to his own plans. And right now, whatever her role in all this, she was off balance. He had to take advantage of that situation as soon as possible. He put the papers into an envelope, then picked up the notebook Paul had slipped him at the arena.

Next to the combination to his own safe, Paul had written another set of numbers Simon knew well. Lumped together as they were, they meant nothing. Separated in the right way, they were highway and rural route numbers leading to a secluded mountain cabin in the Colorado Rocky Mountains, property that had been in the Taylor family for seven generations.

That was where his brother had chosen to wait, and in a matter of hours Simon would be by his side. He pulled out of his driveway shortly after midnight, looking like a fisherman getting a very early start, but not even the mysterious Jessie McMillan was there to see him go.

Jessie was feeling anything but mysterious. She felt like a fool, and was taking it out on the only one who would listen at this hour.

"Well, I don't think it's funny at all, Miles," she said tersely.

Over the phone, along with the slight buzz of static, Jessie could hear the high-rolling activity of a casino in the background. It did little for her disposition. While she sat in a lonely hotel room, confused and frustrated, Miles was in Las Vegas, drink in hand and having the time of his life.

"I still don't see why you're so upset," he replied in a soothing tone. "You knew before you left New York that your cover as an antique dealer would wear thin in a hurry. Now you've got another one, and I might add that your cover as a thief is one you've grown pretty comfortable with over the years."

"I suppose," she said glumly. "It just galls me, that's all. I can't believe someone ratted on me. What happened to honor among thieves?"

"That's a myth and you know it. Besides, I imagine your Simon Taylor got his misinformation from a representative of the black market. There's precious little honor among that crowd at the best of times."

Jessie felt irritable and grouchy. "He's not *my* Simon Taylor."

"My, aren't we touchy? Just why are you so

worried about him thinking you a thief, then?" Miles asked.

Good question. Deep down she knew that was the cause of her sour mood: What must Simon think of her now? She would much rather have him know she was after his brother. The truth would be much easier to explain than the lie he now believed.

Still, she hadn't really even admitted her feelings to herself yet, let alone Miles. "I'm not worried about what he thinks. It's just that now I won't be able to get within a hundred yards of him without him running in the other direction."

Miles wasn't through probing her emotions. "And that's what really bothers you, right? Not being able to see him again, except through a pair of binoculars."

"Stop it, Miles," Jessie demanded. "The fact that Simon thinks I'm a burglar just makes my job harder, that's all. I want to wrap this mess up quickly."

"So you can prove to him you're on the side of good instead of evil?"

"Damn it!" Jessie had to take a deep breath before she could continue. She had no reason to yell at Miles. He was jealous, she could hear it in his voice. And he was absolutely right. Finishing this job meant more to her now than simply collecting a fee. "What do you hear from the network?" she asked, changing the subject.

Miles took the hint, but his voice still held an infuriating, know-it-all quality. "Nothing as yet. But call me again tomorrow. I'm expecting a report from our brokerage friend in New York. The firm Paul Taylor worked for is being awfully quiet about all of this, and I don't like it one bit."

"No, neither do I. I'll be on surveillance again tomorrow, but I'll take a break around noon and call you."

"Sounds good," Miles replied. "And Jessie?"

"Yes?"

"You might consider the fact that Simon did release you as being a good sign. I mean, you said he knows where you're staying, right? Any cops knocking on your door?"

"No," she admitted. But the thought had occurred to her. She had only returned to her room to pack and call Miles. She'd be leaving as soon as she hung up. "All that probably means is he doesn't want the police around asking questions." Still, she wouldn't go back to her post outside Simon's house until morning, just in case. "All he's really got on me is a trespassing charge. That's a pretty minor problem compared to the situation he's involved in."

"Quit being so logical. This is hard enough for me to say as it is. Maybe Simon doesn't have any desire to see you in jail," he said sadly. "Maybe he has desires in other directions."

"Miles . . ."

"Lord, who could blame him? Take care, Jessie."

Leaving the hotel, Jessie kept an eye out for the police, but somehow knew it was unnecessary. She still felt Simon had let her go because he couldn't be bothered. But there had been a look in his eyes when he had let go of her arm and realized she was running away. It had been a look of anger, certainly, but with just a hint of pain and betrayal, and it haunted her the rest of the night.

As she drove past Simon's house early the next morning, the first thing Jessie saw wiped the last sleepy cobweb from her mind and brought her full awake. His car was gone.

A vehicle she hadn't seen before had taken its place in the driveway, and an uneasy feeling made her pull in behind the strange car. Muttering choice expletives under her breath, Jessie knocked on the front door, already knowing what she would find and furious with herself.

A petite Vietnamese woman answered the door, her wizened face curious but cautious. "Yes?"

"Is Simon here?" She knew he wasn't, but perhaps she could get his housekeeper to let her inside for a look around, get some clue as to where he had gone. "I was swimming with him yesterday and forgot my—"

"Yes. You left borrowed suit on floor. Wet."

So much for claiming the suit to be hers and for getting the woman to trust her. "Sorry. Is Simon here?"

"He has gone fishing."

"Where?"

The woman shrugged. "He left a mess too. Clothes everywhere," she replied. She looked Jessie up and down, then laughed with great amusement. "His suitcase is gone. Maybe he will find another fish, one who does not leave suit on floor." Then she closed the door, bringing an end to the conversation.

Jessie got back in her car and drove away, not knowing where she was going or what to do now. His suitcase gone, clothes all over. He had evidently taken off in a hurry, and it sounded like he planned to be gone for some time. Either her nocturnal visit last night had spooked him, or he suspected her of being more than a common thief and had left in a rush to catch her off guard.

If so, he had accomplished his task. She had no idea where he had gone and no clues to follow. She had wasted precious time playing cat and mouse, had allowed this insane attraction to him to interfere with her judgment every step of the way. Now he had outsmarted her, and she

110

prayed he hadn't outsmarted himself as well. A little voice inside her head kept telling her Simon was about to step into more trouble than he could deal with.

She went back to the little motel room she had checked in to late last night and called Miles. A terrible thought had implanted itself in her mind, and as she listened to his report, her uneasiness grew.

"Something's wrong, Jessie." His voice sounded as worried as she felt. "It's all very smooth and quiet, but Paul's former associates have definitely arranged a nasty surprise for him."

"I see. Local talent?"

"No. Chicago, I think. As I said, they're being very cagey about the arrangements."

"Why now?" Jessie wondered aloud. "According to Harrold Stone, they made some cursory attempts to locate Paul when he first disappeared, then gave up."

"Maybe they were waiting for things to calm down," Miles suggested. "Not such a bad idea when you think about it. Take the heat off, let Taylor think they had lost interest or something, then wait for him to go to ground somewhere."

Jessie stretched out on the hard motel bed, trying to make her mind work. "Let's think this through, Miles. You and I know Paul's old firm hasn't forgotten about him, and I don't think he would assume that either."

"I suppose not," Miles agreed.

"Then why would he settle anywhere? He would know the longer he stayed in one place, the greater the chance someone would find him."

"We don't really know that he *has* settled, Jessie," he pointed out.

"No, but this sudden activity from his pals points in that direction. For the sake of argument, let's say he has stopped running for the moment. Why?"

"Could be he's cocky or just plain stupid."

"No. Neither of the Taylor brothers are stupid. Lacking in common sense, perhaps, but not dumb."

Miles sighed. "You've got something in mind, Jessie. Why don't you just come out and say it?"

"Because I want to see if you come to the same conclusion. I haven't been doing too well in the logic department lately," she explained.

"Okay. The only reason I can think of for Paul to stay in one spot is that he's waiting for something."

"Or someone?"

He chuckled. "I think your logic is just fine, dear," Miles assured her. "That's where Simon took off to in such a hurry. I don't see what good it'll do either of them, though. It'll just give the boys from Chicago another target."

Jessie closed her eyes and swallowed hard. The same thought was plaguing her. She managed to close off her fear and continue. "What if there's more to it than brotherly camaraderie in a time of need? What if Paul has an ace up his sleeve?"

"Such as?"

"Paul brought a very big deal to a screeching halt by absconding with funds allocated for certain stock transactions. But it wasn't the money he was after. He gave that back."

"I thought you said he wasn't stupid."

"Now, Miles. Not everyone has your highly developed sense of avarice," she chastised. "I'm working on the assumption he found himself involved in something he didn't want any part in. The only way he could think of to extricate himself was to stop the deal cold, then take off."

"But he must have known that wouldn't be the end of it, right?"

"Right. So he prepared for the inevitable backlash."

"I've got it!" Miles interjected excitedly. "He's got the skinny on his business partners, information that would ensure his survival should they decide to seek revenge. But why didn't he just take it to the cops or the SEC?"

"Think about it, Miles. Paul's no boy scout. He

was happily going along with the whole thing, then developed cold feet. He's guilty of complicity if nothing else."

"Boy. 'Oh what a tangled web we weave . . .'"

"He's an amateur at deception, that's for sure," Jessie agreed. "I think things moved too fast for him at the end. He left his information in a safe place, then couldn't get to it before they started trailing him."

"And that's where Simon fits in," he said. "He's playing the role of courier."

"Go to the head of the class, Miles dear. I certainly don't belong there. I should have figured this all out a long time ago," Jessie said in self-derision. "Once Paul has the information, he'll probably set something up where any attempt to silence him will cause the scheme to be made public."

Miles gave a long, low whistle. "Jessie, if they've figured out where Paul is and get to him before he can arrange his insurance policy . . ."

Again Jessie felt the icy hand of fear. "I know. And if they do know where he is, and have figured out the same thing we just have, then Simon is probably walking into a trap."

"What are you going to do?"

What I should have been doing from the beginning, Jessie thought, *instead of developing an infatuation for a man who was one step ahead of me all the way.* "My job, Miles. I'm supposed to be a hotshot, and it's high time I started living up to my reputation."

"Would you step out of the car please, sir?"

"I wasn't speeding, Officer," Simon said irritably.

"I didn't say you were." The policeman's voice, though polite, definitely held an edge of tension. "Just get out of the car and keep your hands where I can see them."

Simon was transfixed by the piercing beam of a spotlight, combining with the headlights of the patrol car to make the gloom of evening almost bright as day. The officer's service revolver was still holstered, but the safety strap was undone, and his hand rested lightly on the grip. He decided he had better do as he was told.

He couldn't believe this. Except for an interminably long stretch of highway through the Texas Panhandle, he had observed the speed limit and all other rules of the road. The last thing he had wanted was to be delayed in some backwater town in the wee hours of the morning. He had even stopped in Amarillo and checked into a motel for a few hours' sleep, then grabbed some lunch and plenty of coffee to fuel him for the last leg of his journey.

Once over Raton Pass and into Colorado, the old feeling of security had returned. He loved

Dallas too, had chosen to make his home there for more reasons than the increased market for his talents as a karate instructor. But Colorado was home. It was Paul's home as well, which probably accounted for his decision to hide out there.

Right outside of Pueblo, Colorado, just as he was in his third chorus of a John Denver classic, the flashing lights of a state patrol car popped his happy bubble. He pulled over and got out his license, prepared for some kind of lecture. State troopers were a conscientious lot, and he couldn't remember if he had signaled a lane change before passing that last car.

Now, much to his confusion, he stood looking into the pale-blue eyes of an edgy two-hundred-fifty–pound patrolman. The man's partner was using the radio, checking license and registration, but his eyes were on Simon as well.

"Uh, what's going on?" Simon asked nervously.

"This vehicle has been reported as stolen."

"There must be some mistake. . . ."

The trooper sighed. Why did they always say that? "Do you own this car?"

"Of course I—"

Finished with the radio, the other officer joined them between the two cars. "Checks out. It's on the sheet, but a Simon Taylor owns it, and this is Simon Taylor."

"Yeah?" His partner seemed doubtful.

"Sure. If you watched more than old movies on the cable, you'd know. He's a top contender on the karate circuit." The man turned to Simon. "What happened in New York last week?"

Simon breathed a sigh of relief. "Exhaustion. That's where I'm headed now, for a little R and R."

"Any idea why someone would report your car stolen?"

"My business manager didn't want me to take this vacation; I suppose this was his way of getting in the last word."

The radio squawked, and both officers turned to leave. "We'll take your plate number off the list," one said as he got into the patrol car. "It takes awhile to get it off of the computer, but I don't think you'll have any more problems."

"Thanks."

"Sorry for the delay. Hope you catch some big ones."

"What?" Simon looked at the fishing gear in his back seat. "Oh. From the feel of this wind, I'll probably end up having to chop a hole in the ice to do it."

"Could be. High country's already had some snow. Drive carefully." They pulled back onto the highway and sped off.

Simon got back in his car and did the same,

but carefully kept the speedometer at fifty-five. "I'll get you for this, Barney," he muttered.

The rest of his trip was relatively uneventful, with the exception of blowing and drifting snow on the high mountain passes. He wended his way carefully into the back country, watching the sparsely populated area grow wilder and wilder by the mile. At last he pulled off onto a rutted dirt road and went down it for a half hour or so until it ended in a rocky gully.

He got out of his car, inhaling the chill air, his breath making puffs of condensation as he shrugged into his backpack. Though the sky held patchy clouds, the moon was full, providing plenty of light. If he had a four-wheel drive, as he could tell Paul did from the recent tracks, he could get to the cabin in a matter of minutes.

As it was he faced a lengthy hike up a slippery rock-strewn slope. It didn't bother him, though. He was dressed for it, and it felt good to be out of the car and stretching his muscles.

The silence stunned him. Only nature's noises broke the quiet; the river roared below him, and small nocturnal animals scurried away from his intrusive presence. When at long last he reached his destination, he was pleasantly tired.

The cabin was rough-hewn and worn by the harsh climate, an appearance that belied the modernization that had taken place inside over the years. A sifting of light snow covered everything, sparkling in the moonlight. The air seemed crystal clear, charged with energy, and Simon could smell wood smoke on the breeze. He smiled, started toward the cabin, then stopped in his tracks. Something was wrong.

Martial arts training developed many things in a person over time, especially with the dedication Simon had. There was nothing supernatural or mystic about it at all. In years of learning how to deal with trouble and violence, Simon had developed a nose for it, could feel it, simply knew when it was around and coming his way. He had that feeling now.

There was no one in sight. Paul would have been watching for Simon even at this late hour and would have greeted him. The door to the cabin was closed. There were lights glowing inside, but the curtains on the windows were drawn shut. Simon slipped into the trees lining the path on either side of him. He had to decide whether to wait for something to happen or to take the initiative and go in for a closer look. The vagaries of Rocky Mountain weather made his decision for him. It began to drizzle rain.

Though dressed for the climate, he would soon be wet and shivering, and at this altitude hypothermia would not be far behind. Already tired and chilly, he had to get inside before the cold sapped any more of his strength.

Cautiously he made his way through the pines

to the front porch, then skirted it and headed for the back door, keeping low so he couldn't be seen through the windows. Now, close to the thick, heavily insulated walls of the cabin, he could hear sounds from within, and they didn't please him. Someone was either ransacking the place or having a knock-down, drag-out fight. Whichever, he had to go in and put a stop to it. He put his hand on the door knob and collected his concentration.

At the end of his patience and his reserve of body heat, Simon burst through the back door and ran right into a big, barrel-chested man in a bulky red coat. The impact doubled the man over, and Simon helped him along by lifting his knee sharply. The man went down on the floor in a heap.

Then Simon stopped moving, because he noticed he had also run into the bane of any hand-to-hand combat situation: another man of similar size, pointing a forty-five–caliber automatic handgun in his direction.

The man Simon had hit was on the floor, moaning. The other didn't seem to notice. "Look here, Dan. A visitor."

Simon's eyes were mere slits. He was ready to knock the man at his feet down again should he try to get up, but he kept his arms relaxed at his sides and his attention focused on the man with the gun.

"Who the hell are you?" he asked. "Where's Paul?"

"Both very good questions. As a matter of fact, I was about to ask them myself," the man replied.

"What have you done with my brother?" Simon demanded.

"Very good," he said condescendingly. "Two questions answered in one breath. You are Simon Taylor, and you don't know where that slimy coward is either. Well, never mind." He spoke to his partner, but his eyes never left Simon. "Get up, Dan, and relieve Mr. Taylor of his burden."

"I think he broke my ribs," Dan complained but did the other's bidding. Simon let him take the backpack. He couldn't do much else, looking down a gun barrel as he was.

The one called Dan dumped the contents of the pack out on the floor, where it joined a great quantity of broken furniture and other household paraphernalia. He picked out the envelope with Paul's papers in it, examined the contents briefly, then held it up in triumph.

"He brought us a present," he announced.

"How nice." The gun in his hand never wavering, the other man stepped closer to Simon. "I bet you'd like to take this from me and shove it down my throat, wouldn't you, Mr. Kung Fu?" He punctuated his insult by jabbing the auto-

121

matic into Simon's stomach. "And you know what? I'm smart enough to realize you could probably do it." He stepped back and nodded slightly to Dan.

"Now?" Dan asked.

"In a second. We'll find your brother for you, Mr. Kung Fu, but right now we have enough to keep our finicky employer happy. Maybe he'll even give us a big fat bonus, right, Dan?"

Dan grunted and picked up the thick leg of a broken chair, hefting it like a club. Simon's body tensed instinctively, coiling like a spring. He knew beyond a shadow of a doubt he could knock both of these men to their knees before they even knew what hit them. Bare-handed, neither of them stood a chance against his highly trained reflexes. But a gun was the ultimate equalizer, as Simon was very much aware. The big barrel of the automatic was pointed directly at him.

Still, he probably would have tried it anyway if he thought they were about to kill him. But his finely honed instincts in such matters told him that wasn't the case. His feeling was confirmed by the man with the gun.

"Careful, Mr. Kung Fu." He lifted the gun and pointed it right between Simon's eyes. "You weren't in our plans, but that doesn't mean we won't change those plans just for you." An evil smile spread across his face. He chewed tobacco; Simon could see a big wad of it in his cheek.

"What do you want from me?" Simon asked.

"Either you let Dan whack you on the head, or we'll see if you're faster than a speeding bullet."

Simon glared at him. "Mind if I say something first?"

"Why not?"

"I'll bet the girls just go wild over those brown teeth of yours."

He had the satisfaction of seeing the man scowl angrily just before the room exploded into stars.

CHAPTER SEVEN

.

Someone was opening Simon's eyes. It certainly wasn't his idea. He felt like he was floating, and the darkness was his friend. A light flashed across his foggy field of vision, on and off, first one eye, then the other. Once he became aware that he had arms and legs, he felt something warm pressing against his wrist. Then he wished that whoever was bothering him had left him alone, because he noticed his head felt like it was about to fall off.

"What do you see?" a soft, worried voice asked.

He tried to focus on the movement in front of his face. "Fingers," he replied, then wished he hadn't. Moving his jaw made his whole body hurt.

"That's a start. How many?"

It took a great effort to remember how to count. "Six?"

"Try again."

Simon blinked. That hurt too, but his vision cleared at last. "Three," he said with more conviction. He saw three fingers. Three beautiful, soft, feminine fingers. He turned his head to try to see whom they belonged to and nearly blacked out again.

"Who are you? Jessie! . . . What—how did you find . . ."

"I wouldn't try to move just yet," Jessie cautioned. "I don't think you have a concussion, but somebody sure gave it a good try."

"Your turn," Simon said weakly. "How many heads do I have?"

Jessie smiled, her concern evident in her voice. "Just one, though you've got a lump that will probably get big enough to qualify as another." She examined it gingerly, wincing in sympathy right along with him. "I'm going to have to clean this up, but I'd like to get you off of the floor first. Think you can make it?"

"Nope." He started to shake his head no and immediately thought better of it. "I sort of like it here, thank you."

He was quite a man. With the wound he had received she couldn't imagine how he was speaking, let alone making jokes. She gently stroked his face, feeling a spark kindle deep within her. Though she had considerable first-aid training, she had never been much of a nurse. But the thought of taking care of Simon gave her great pleasure.

"It's cold in here, and the floor is even colder. I've got to get you up and I can't do it without your help," she informed him.

"Cold?" Simon tried to remember how he had come to be lying there. "There was a fire going, and two men . . ."

"Whoever hit you is long gone, and the fire must have gone out hours ago. It's morning, Simon."

"Morning?" That couldn't be. He looked toward the window across from him and saw the first hint of gray light signaling a new day. "I got here around midnight." His sluggish mind tried to make some sense out of what had happened.

"It's a little before six now."

"Paul—"

"First we take care of you, then we'll worry about your brother." She slipped her arm under his neck. "Try to sit up, and we'll take it from there."

Simon gritted his teeth and did as she said, holding back a wave of nausea. To his surprise it passed quickly, and with his arm around her shoulder he stood up and made it to the couch in front of the fireplace. He felt stiff and creaky. The couch was soft beneath him as he stretched out and waited for the room to stop spinning.

Jessie disappeared for a few moments and

came back with a first-aid kit. "This is going to hurt."

"Then you won't mind if I scream?"

"I can take it if you can."

Once clean, his wound didn't look as bad as she had first feared. She applied a dressing and bandaged his head, then gave him some aspirin. A few embers still glowed in the fireplace. With a little effort she managed to get a fire going again then returned to his side, removed his hiking boots, and pulled a quilt over him. Carefully she sat down next to his reclining form, her expression curious.

"How do you feel now?" Jessie asked.

"Better. Thanks." He looked into those beautiful eyes of hers, felt himself grow warm at the concern he saw there.

"Feel up to telling me what happened?"

Simon's expression became guarded. He had a few questions himself. "I came up here to meet my brother. We were going to do a little fishing and—"

"Simon," Jessie said, cutting him off by putting a finger to his lips. "The time has come for truth. I know why you came here. I know about the trouble Paul is in, probably know more about this whole thing than you do."

His eyes narrowed. "Maybe you even know the guys who tried to bash my skull in," he said bitterly.

"No." She sighed and brushed a lock of hair from his forehead. He pushed her hand away. "No, I don't know them. But I know who sent them, and why."

He struggled to sit upright. Jessie put a cushion behind him so he could. He was very angry, but it was good to see the color returning to his face. And after all, he had a perfect right to be mad at her and the whole world just now.

"Who the hell *are* you?" he demanded.

"I'm a . . ." A what? Private detective? Bounty hunter? "I find things. People sometimes. Sometimes I just find things out about people," she explained. "I was hired to find your brother, to help get him out of the mess he's gotten himself into. You've got to believe me, Simon. I want to help Paul, not hurt him."

"So you're not a thief." Simon grimaced in distaste. "Why should I believe you? Everything you've done and said so far has been a lie. Hasn't it, Jessie?"

She lowered her gaze. "No. Not everything. I meant it when I said I liked you. That was part of the trouble, really. I found myself liking you too much, and it interfered with my job," she replied softly. "I should have been honest with you right from the start, but I was afraid of what you might think of me."

"I don't think too much of you now, lady."

The roughness in his voice caused her a great

deal of pain. She tried not to lash out at him, but couldn't help it. "I suppose you would have preferred it if I left you on the floor?" she asked angrily. "Cold, unconscious, with a gash in your head? Maybe I should just leave you to fend for yourself." She stood up, her hands on her hips, looking down at him with a defiant air. "You've done such a good job of that so far."

Simon glared at her, then pulled her back down to sit beside him. "Oh, shut up," he said contritely. He looked at the fury in her eyes, decided he liked her smile much better. "I'm sorry. It does look like you're a heck of a lot better at this than I am. How *did* you find me?"

"It wasn't easy," Jessie admitted. Slowly her scowl was replaced with a wry grin. "I got lucky, really. I managed to get a list of telephone calls to and from your suite in New York. One of them was from a pay phone at Denver Stapleton Airport. Then I had the tax records searched to see if you or Paul owned property here and tracked down the location of this place."

Simon was listening intently, fascinated by the process. "But you couldn't be sure Paul was here, or that I was coming here."

"I wasn't, but it became a pretty good bet, thanks to the Colorado State Patrol and the contact report they logged on you. That was the lucky part. If you had been stopped in Texas or New Mexico—"

"You reported my car stolen!" Simon exclaimed.

Jessie nodded sheepishly. "I have a friend in Dallas who works at city hall."

Suddenly Simon was angry all over again. "Then why didn't you tell them everything, have me detained or something?" He gingerly touched the bandage on his head.

"Simon," she said gently, "I'm not a licensed private investigator. I'm a private party who does work for other private parties. Why do you think I was hired to find your brother? Why do you think the police aren't involved in this?" Jessie watched his anger turn to confusion. "You don't even really know what Paul has done, do you?"

"No."

She told him all the facts she knew and the educated guesses she had made so far. He confirmed those guesses by telling her his side, from Paul's first phone call to the events of the previous night. Finally she saw the light of understanding dawn in his eyes. Along with it she saw self-disgust and despair.

"And I let him down," he said. "I was supposed to be bringing him his insurance policy, and I let the other side take it away from me."

"I don't think you had much choice," Jessie said sympathetically. "If you're going to blame anyone, blame me. I was the one who let you get away, lined you up for a bump on the head by keeping quiet," she added, angry with herself for allowing Simon to get hurt. "I thought I could handle it by myself."

Simon reached out and touched her cheek. "No. Thank you for not calling the police. Those guys didn't want me, they wanted Paul and the papers." He chuckled, but without much humor. "I just got in the way."

"At least they didn't get Paul. Now I've got to find him before they do. Without those papers he's a sitting duck."

"You mean *we've* got to find him, don't you?"

"No, Simon," she answered strongly. "Those guys let you off easy this time because you're not really involved. But you go traipsing around getting in their way again and they may very well add you to their list."

"He's my brother, Jessie. I'm going."

Jessie could almost feel the determination in him. But this was a pointless conversation. She could remind him that he was in no condition to go anywhere, and he would deny it. She could tell him that she was a professional and this was her job, but he wouldn't listen. To debate the matter further would only put him on his guard and make it harder for her to slip away.

The feelings she had for him were growing by the moment, with every touch and every word. The fact of the matter was, he wasn't going anywhere, at least not with her, because she wouldn't let him. There was no way she was going to put him in any more jeopardy.

"Hey, take it easy," Jessie said, her tone easy and lighthearted. "We'll talk about it later. I've been up most of the night and I would hardly call what you had sleep." She stood up, smiling at him, then looked around. "Point me in the direction of the kitchen and I'll rustle us up some breakfast, then we'll both get a few hours of much-needed rest."

Simon pointed the way. He was feeling much better, even quite hungry, but couldn't deny the drowsiness in his own voice. "What about Paul? We have to get after him."

"Do you have any idea where he might have gone?"

"Well, no, but—"

"Neither do I. I do, however, have a pretty good information network. I found you, didn't I?"

Simon smiled back at her. "Yes. And thank you again, Jessie."

"My pleasure," she replied, a bit startled at the sensuality in her voice. She cleared her throat and tried to look stern. "Just let me do my job."

He sighed. "Okay, mystery woman." He leaned back on the couch and closed his eyes.

Jessie had to wake him up to feed him, then

checked on him occasionally as she worked the last of her nervous energy out by picking up the house. He slept deeply but normally, not the sleep of concussion. At last she curled up in a cozy overstuffed chair next to the fire.

Simon had been knocked around a bit in his career and obviously recovered quickly from such rough treatment. Jessie could tell this by the way he was nibbling on her neck when she woke up.

"Mmm," he hummed appreciatively. "You taste good."

No sooner was she fully awake than she felt her body coming alive beneath his gentle touch. He was sitting on the ottoman she had her legs stretched out on, and his hands were beneath her blanket, exploring the curves of her hips.

"H-how's the head?" she managed to ask.

"Thick, evidently. Stings a little is all."

Jessie shivered as his tongue outlined the shell of her ear. "You get well awfully quick."

"It's an overabundance of hormones," he murmured. He trailed kisses across her cheek, then softly brushed her lips with his. "They make wounds heal faster."

His hands, warm and sure, wandered up her rib cage. She gasped at his bold touch, her nipples hardening under his palms even through the thick flannel of her shirt. A fire was glowing to life within her, and she had no intention of stopping it. She wanted Simon every bit as much as he so obviously wanted her.

"Shouldn't you be lying down?" she asked, her voice hoarse and barely above a whisper.

"I think we both should." He scooped her up, proving both his strength and his fitness. His lips found hers and claimed them as his own as he put her down on the couch and gently settled himself full length beside her. "Better?"

Jessie opened her mouth to speak and he filled it with his tongue, sweet, soft, and demanding, drinking her in like vintage champagne. His hand roamed over her jeans-clad thighs, up the gentle mound of her stomach, and on to cup each swelling breast in turn. She moaned, a warmth spreading through her, a tingling sensation along all her nerve endings from head to toe. She shivered and he wrapped her into his arms, giving his heat, communicating his need.

Strong, hard, and masculine, his every inch pressed against her, telling her of power and desire held barely in check. Jessie's own desire surged near the surface, leaping at his touch as his deft fingers sought first the buttons of her shirt, the catch of her bra, then the zipper of her jeans. He stroked her, explored her, cherishing the weight of her breasts in his hand. Their lips met, their tongues danced, words forgotten in favor of another, infinitely more intimate language. Simon tasted her, delicately circling the aroused peak of each breast before sucking her greedily into his mouth.

As Jessie removed his shirt and pressed herself against him, she thought back to the first time he had touched her, kissed her. From that moment on, she realized, the die had been cast. Their desire for each other was like an unquenchable thirst, one they tried to satisfy with feverish abandon. Clothes were a frustration soon removed, discarded in a tangle on the floor. The blazing fire beside them warmed their skin but couldn't match the flames from within that threatened to consume them in their passionate embrace.

Simon was strong yet gentle, his touch soft yet demanding as he explored Jessie's every curve, learning the secret places that made her moan or cry out in joy, her every sigh sweet music to his ears. Jessie returned his caresses in kind, discovering ways to make his body tremble beneath her hands. Her passion made her bold. She traced the taut outlines of his stomach with her tongue and reveled in his shuddering reaction, nipping at him with her teeth, feeling him grow hard beneath her fluttering fingertips.

Rolling atop her, probing tenderly and with concern, Simon found her ready and willing to accept the consequences of her teasing. He filled her slowly, felt her surround him, their voices blending in pleasure and delight as their bodies became one. Jessie clung to him, matched his growing rhythm, felt his strength inside her and met it with her own. They were buffeted by a need delayed too long, mindless and lost in each other's arms, a delicious torture from which they sought release and yet wished could go on forever.

A wave of pleasure pursued and finally overtook the lovers, held them in its grasp and touched their every fiber, then sent them tumbling one after another over the edge into a soft and peaceful cloud. Nestled in Simon's arms, Jessie drifted off to sleep as he held and stroked her, the warmth of their lovemaking settling around her like a glow.

Just before noon the black storm clouds that had been threatening all morning gave way to azure skies, leaving only damp ground and a definite nip in the air as a reminder. Jessie and Simon stood on the front porch of the cabin, looking out at the mountain vista around them.

Simon wrapped his arms around her from behind and kissed the nape of her neck. "Lovely."

"Yes, it is." She leaned against him and put her hands on his.

"I wasn't talking about the view."

Jessie tilted her head and kissed him. "I think you're fully recuperated," she teased.

"I am. Want me to show you?"

"Aren't you forgetting something?" Jessie asked. "Like Paul, for instance?"

"I know," Simon replied, serious now. "I wish he'd learn to keep his nose clean. He was always in some kind of trouble, even in school. Money, women. Maybe this will scare him into seeing that fast bucks are usually illegal ones."

She turned and looked at him uncertainly. "Simon, I told you I want to help him, and I do. But you realize he won't come out of this smelling like a rose, don't you?"

"What's that supposed to mean?"

Jessie could see the old tension return to him, saw the protectiveness in his eyes. "This deal he got involved in. It's beginning to look more complicated than it appeared at first. The man who hired me and I will do everything we can, but Paul may very well end up in jail."

"But he backed out!" Simon exclaimed angrily. "If he cooperates with the law . . ."

"We don't know if he's willing to do that, now do we?" she pointed out. "I'm just telling it like it is. He should have gone to the Securities and Exchange Commission at the first hint of illegality, but he didn't. He should have taken the information he had and turned it over to them instead of taking the matter into his own hands, but he didn't." Jessie reached out and put a hand on his arm. "Even now, without his trump card,

I'm willing to bet he's still running instead of owning up to the fact that he's in over his head."

"I thought you said you wanted to help him," Simon said accusingly.

"I do, Simon. I'll do everything I can. But he's got to stop running, he's got to come in before he gets hurt, maybe killed."

Simon sighed heavily, running his hands over his face. "You're right. I'm sorry." He looked at her, into those eyes that had smoldered with such passion a short time ago. "I wish none of this was happening. I wish we could stay here forever, make love and forget about the world."

"Oh, Simon," Jessie replied, stepping closer to him and touching his cheek. "I wish we could too." She hugged him, grinning impishly. "But look at it this way. If Paul hadn't gotten into trouble, we wouldn't have met."

Simon grinned and hugged her back. "Good point. I'm afraid for him, but I suppose I should thank him for getting me involved in all this. I will, when I see him."

"Me too. Now," she said, heading back inside and tugging him along, "let's get our things together and get going."

"What do you say we come back here, after this is all over?" He pulled her into his arms again. "Bring a month's worth of food and let the world go by?"

It sounded wonderful, more tempting than he

138

knew. But she knew there were many pitfalls between now and then. He wouldn't like being left behind when she located Paul, had already seen how he felt about his brother being locked up for his part in this deal. How would he feel about her, knowing she had been instrumental in bringing Paul to justice? She could only hope he would be happy his brother was alive and grateful for her help.

"I'd like that, Simon. I can't think of anything I'd rather do than be with you, here or anywhere else." She kissed him, then pushed playfully against his chest. "Now, come on! There's work to do."

"Taskmaster."

"That's mistress," she corrected.

"Applying for the job?" Simon's eyebrows bobbed up and down roguishly.

"Would you get a move on?" She tried to sound angry, but the thought gave her a very warm feeling indeed.

They hiked down the mountain to their vehicles. Jessie's was a four-wheel-drive truck she had rented at the airport in Denver. They started their engines and let them warm up. Simon rolled down his window, raising his voice over the noise.

"How did you know which direction to go from here?" he asked curiously.

"I followed your tracks, naturally," she replied.

He laughed. "Naturally. You're something else, Jessie McMillan. Will I ever *really* know you?"

She grinned, her voice playful and sensuous. "You're off to a pretty good start, champ."

Since Simon knew the route so well, he led and Jessie followed back to the main highway. Then, however, she knew where she was and what had to be done. She had to call Miles and get back on Paul's trail. But first she had to get rid of Simon. He would stick to her like glue once they got down out of these mountains and into Denver, and she couldn't allow that.

Whether he liked it or not, Jessie was going to keep him out of harm's way from then on. Wherever Paul had gone, danger was close behind him. Jessie was used to danger. She was paid for putting herself in its path. Despite his physical prowess, Simon would just get in her way. She would be too worried about him to concentrate on the job at hand, and that would be bad for his brother, for her, and for him.

She was concerned for Paul, but she was more concerned for Simon. It wasn't something she was prepared to think about too deeply yet, but she knew she was falling in love.

It was a simple task to lose Simon in the hustle of Denver traffic. Jessie had a feel for cities.

Plunked down anywhere in a large town, she could find her way around almost like a native. She had told Simon she was going to the airport, not an out-and-out lie since she might very well end up there. First she checked in to a motel near the airport and got down to business.

"Hello, Miles. Sorry to pull you away from the roulette table."

"Hah! Roulette is for fools." His voice crackled disdainfully over the phone lines. "Blackjack's my game."

"Besides, the blackjack dealers are cute, right?"

"You know there's only one woman for me," he replied in a playful tone.

"Better look again," Jessie said without thinking.

Miles sighed resignedly. "I take it you found your missing paramour?"

"He's not my . . ." Why fight it? Her denial sounded hollow even to her. "I didn't call to discuss my liaisons. We've got trouble."

"Don't tell me. Paul's gone, the papers are gone, and you're left holding the, um, bag. So to speak."

Jessie ignored his taunting innuendo. "Half right. Simon arrived with the papers, but his brother had already flown the coop. Presumably he saw something coming, which is more than can be said for Simon. Two gentlemen from the

141

windy city greeted him with a whack on the head, took the papers, and faded back from whence they came."

"Knocked him on the head, left him for dead, and fled."

"Not funny, Miles."

"Sorry. I mean that, Jessie," he said sincerely —if a bit sadly. "Is Simon all right?"

"He's fine. Wandering around Denver looking for me at the moment, and probably madder than he's ever been, but he'll get over it." *I hope,* she thought.

"Good. And it's good you ditched him, because things are heating up. *You* were only half right in your assessment of the situation as well, dear," Miles informed her with a touch of smugness. "These men who hit Simon. Were they big, burly gentlemen, one with a beard, one a clean-shaven tobacco chewer?"

"I only arrived in time to pick up the pieces, but yes, that sounds like the description Simon gave. Who are they?"

"The Terlin brothers, Mark and Daniel. They hail from Fort Worth, Texas, and belong to a very wealthy rancher, one of the principals in the deal Paul soured," Miles explained. "Evidently he is none too pleased with the way Paul's associates have handled this affair so far and has decided to settle accounts personally."

Jessie nodded. "I thought they handled things

a bit unprofessionally, letting Simon see their faces and leaving him around to tell the tale. Not that I'm ungrateful for their oversight, mind you."

"From what I can tell, they're strictly amateurs," Miles said. "More bully boys than anything. Their boss wanted the papers, which he now has, but he wants Paul too. We haven't heard the last of them, I'm afraid."

"Lovely," Jessie replied sardonically. "But what about the other two?"

"I was getting to that," he answered calmly. "My inquiries into their past have been met with stony silence, which is an answer in itself. Very cool, very professional, and very, very nasty individuals."

"Then why—"

"Why weren't they the first on the scene?" Miles interjected. "They are hunters, dear, pure and simple. As such they prefer the sport of the chase to trapping their quarry in his den."

"They were waiting for Paul to run?"

"Evidently they were aware of the Terlin brothers and used them like bird dogs to flush Paul out into the open. Even as we speak they are hot on his trail."

"How do you know all this?" Jessie asked.

"Some digging, some deduction. It's your network, Jessie, and it's a good one. I'm simply the interpreter."

He was more than that, and he knew it. "You've earned your pay for the year, Miles. Now for your Christmas bonus."

"Pay your travel agent, not me. Following standard procedure I put her on alert the moment Simon disappeared from Dallas, just in case. No Simon Taylor, of course, but who do you think turned up on her computer about five hours ago?"

"You're kidding," she said in disbelief.

"As you said, Paul may not be dumb but he's sadly lacking in common sense. He used a credit card to purchase a ticket to Los Angeles. Round trip, the optimist." There was a pause, then Miles said, "Should be touching down about now."

Jessie thought of Los Angeles, with its maze of freeways and millions of people. It was a good city to get lost in, even if you weren't trying. For his sake she hoped Paul *was* trying, but that had its bad aspects too. How was she going to find him now?

"Hang up, Miles. I have to call the airport."

"Already done. You leave Stapleton in . . . forty-eight minutes," he informed her, then added, "With a stopover in Las Vegas."

Jessie laughed, glad of his efficiency but piqued with him as well. "No, Miles. This isn't in your job description."

"You're good, Jessie, but you don't have eyes

in the back of your head. I'm sure his hunters were watching the passenger lists too and are about an hour behind. Once they deliver the papers to their boss, I imagine the Terlin brothers will be joining the parade as well."

"But—"

"Besides," he interrupted, "I'm the only one who knows how to contact the shadow I had waiting for Paul at L. A. International."

"You suckered me into this!" she cried.

"And I'm not going to tell you," Miles continued, "until we're both standing on California soil. Or should I say concrete?"

"You are the sneakiest person I ever met!"

Miles sniffed haughtily. "I take that as a compliment, coming from you. Now hang up or you'll be late for your flight."

CHAPTER EIGHT

Waiting in an airport had its hazards, Simon found, especially when one wasn't standing in line for a ticket or sitting restlessly near a boarding gate. He was lingering across the hall from a rental car agency and so far had been approached by several panhandlers, two political activists, and a handful of religious fanatics.

Trying to look unapproachable, he leaned against the wall reading a newspaper, feeling like some streetcorner lookout in a Humphrey Bogart movie. He was also feeling rather proud of himself.

When Jessie's rented truck had disappeared from his rearview mirror, Simon first thought she had gotten lost. After a brief wait by the side of the road and a panicked search of nearby back streets, however, he realized she had gotten lost all right—on purpose. That was when he decided two could play this detective game.

Remembering a bumper sticker on the truck

146

advertising the name of the rental agency, he raced to the airport and questioned one of the girls behind the counter. They did have two such trucks, but both were already out. Simon had thanked her and taken up this post across from the place, playing a hunch that Jessie would show up to return the vehicle. He hoped it was soon, because even with his suitcase beside him he felt anything but inconspicuous.

"Can you help me out, mister?"

Simon looked up from his paper and saw a young man standing there. His attire looked properly pitiful, but something about his air of destitution didn't quite ring true.

"I don't know what school turns you guys out," Simon remarked, "but they should teach you to take off your Rolex before begging money from strangers."

The young man blushed but wasn't easily put off. "It was a gift. I'm trying to raise enough money to—"

"Make the next payment on your Porsche?" Simon offered.

"To get to San Diego so I can—"

"Close the deal on some beachfront property, right?"

"Give me a break." He glared angrily at Simon. "At least I'm not on welfare."

Simon grinned. "You probably make too much to qualify, but at least that's a refreshing approach." He reached into his pocket and gave him a quarter.

"You made me work so hard for this?" the young man asked sarcastically. With a defiant movement he removed his watch, slipped it into his pocket, then spun on his heel and walked away.

Simon sighed and turned back to the rental counter.

His heart raced when he saw her, her black hair shining, long legs and shapely buttocks encased in tight-fitting jeans. Her scent was still with him, the feel of her body molding to his seemed burned into his memory. As hard as it was to do, he stayed where he was, watching from behind his newspaper as Jessie hurriedly transacted her business.

Simon loved the way she walked, so graceful and with an athletic bounce to her stride. He watched her as she headed down the corridor toward the airline ticket counters, following just closely enough to keep her swaying hips in sight. She picked up her ticket, paused for a moment to get her bearings, then took off in the direction of the boarding gates.

"Excuse me," Simon asked the man who had given Jessie her ticket. "Could you tell me if Jessie McMillan has picked up her ticket to Albuquerque yet?"

The man blinked. "Well, she just picked up a

ticket, but it was first class to Los Angeles," he said, craning his neck and looking in the direction Jessie had gone. "She went—"

"Los Angeles?" Simon interrupted with a scowl. "Oh, brother, they must have changed the meeting place at the last second again." He looked at the man hopefully. "Could you sell me a ticket on that flight? See, Jessie's my boss, and she'll kill me if I don't make that meeting."

"They'll be boarding in fifteen minutes. I think it's completely booked . . ."

"I tell you," Simon continued in disgust, "they treat us middle managers like dirt. There was probably a memo telling of the change, but did I get a copy? No." He waved his hands in the air, his voice rising in panic. "I'll lose my job! And Mary Ann just got her braces!"

People were starting to stare. The ticket agent bent over his computer terminal. "Stay calm, sir. If anyone can get you to Los Angeles on time, we can," he said loudly enough for his supervisor to hear.

"If you can, I'll never fly another airline again," Simon told him gratefully. He turned to the curious onlookers and grinned. "This company's the best, isn't it?"

There was a murmur of agreement, then scattered applause when the agent announced, "Yes! We have a cancellation. It's in smoking, though. The other end of the plane from your boss."

"Anything is fine. Thank you!"

He took Simon's name and credit card, then proceeded to write out a ticket in record time. As he handed it to him, however, a frown creased his brow. "Simon Taylor." He muttered the name over a few times and peered at Simon's face. "Wait a minute. Aren't you—"

"Good-bye, and thanks again," Simon said quickly as he dashed off.

After passing through security Simon also passed right by his assigned boarding gate, staying hidden in the crowd. Then he turned and milled about for a moment or two, pretending to look at a photographic display of air force jets, all the while keeping Jessie in sight. When she got up and went to the restroom, he slipped over to the flight attendant near the boarding ramp, limping dramatically. He showed him his ticket. "Yes, sir, you're in the right place. We'll be boarding in a few minutes. If you'll just have a seat . . ."

Simon patted his thigh and smiled apologetically. "I wonder if I might board now? I hurt my leg a week ago and all this walking is getting to me."

"Certainly, sir." He took Simon's carry-on bag and led him down the ramp. "Say, aren't you Simon Taylor, the karate champion?"

Simon glanced over his shoulder and saw Jessie returning to her seat in the waiting area. He limped faster. "Yeah, that's me. Boy, this leg is killing me."

"Have you in your seat in a second. Watch your step."

It was a normal flight, with the exception of a stop in Las Vegas Simon hadn't known about. But he wasn't complaining. He needed the quiet time to think.

Why had Jessie tried to lose him? All sorts of reasons came to mind, the most comforting of which was that she didn't want him getting whacked on the head again. Wonderful, compassionate—and passionate—lady that she was, he'd like to believe that was the answer. But something wouldn't let him.

She had lied to him before, and all romantic notions aside, it was entirely possible she had done so again. She said she wanted to help Paul, but she had also admitted she might not be able to keep him out of trouble with the law. Maybe she viewed bringing Paul to justice as helping him, but Simon certainly didn't.

Paul had a penchant for being in the wrong place at the wrong time, and certainly had more than his fair share of greed, but he wasn't a criminal. Simon felt in his heart that his brother wasn't running just from his former associates, but from himself as well. He had finally gotten himself involved in something illegal, and it had scared him. With a little luck and a chance to start over, Simon felt sure Paul would never play fast and loose with the rules again. He was determined to give his brother that chance.

Only one thing stood in the way of that goal: Jessie. She had been hired to find Paul, that much was certain. But what was she supposed to do with him once she had found him?

Despite his strong feelings for her, he couldn't help thinking that she had given him the slip because she wanted him out of the way. Not because she was worried for his safety, but because she didn't want him interfering with her work. What troubled him the most was that he had no idea whose side she was really on.

Simon wanted to keep the police out of this just as much as Jessie apparently did, but their lack of involvement worried him all the same. What if the people she wanted to turn Paul over to had motives even she didn't know about? She seemed concerned with Paul's safety, but how far did that concern go? Just until she had found him? Only until she had collected her pay?

He had held her in his arms, made love to her, even felt as though a bond had been formed between them that went much deeper than the mutual desire they shared. But he didn't really know her. Maybe he never would. That left him with only one thing to do, and he was doing it.

Jessie was good at finding people. He would stay discreetly on her tail until she found Paul, and then he would find some way of whisking his brother away from her. Once Paul was safe, once they had figured a way out of this devilish mess, then and only then could he turn his attention to the woman he was falling in love with.

A voice broke Simon from his inner-directed thoughts. "Ladies and gentlemen, this is your captain speaking. We will be making our final approach to L. A. International in just a few minutes, and at this time we request you observe the no smoking signs and fasten your seat belt. The weather in Los Angeles this evening is a pleasant seventy-two degrees, with scattered showers in the forecast and moderate air quality. We hope you enjoyed your flight. Thank you for flying with us, and we look forward to serving you in the future."

Up in first class, Jessie and Miles pulled their seat belts tighter and prepared for the landing.

"Okay, you can tell me now," she said.

"We haven't touched down yet."

"Miles . . ."

He looked at her and chuckled. "All right. Our man here has a beeper. We just call his service and wait for him to phone us back."

"A shadow with a beeper?" Jessie shook her head in amused disbelief. "Only in California."

As soon as the plane stopped moving they

were out of their seats, Miles grabbing his bag. They joined the passengers in the aisle and moved quickly from the plane into the terminal, too preoccupied to notice the tall blond man in the crowd behind them.

"Shall we call from here?" Jessie asked.

"We'd better," Miles replied, leading the way toward a bank of telephones. "It'll mean waiting by the phones until he gets a chance to call, but we have no idea what direction to go from here." He inserted coins in the slot and dialed a number from memory.

"I agree. I'll go see about the car rental."

Simon covertly watched their exchange as he got a soft drink from a machine nearby. He didn't recognize the man with Jessie. Was this an employee of hers? They appeared more friendly than that. Maybe this was the friend she had spoken of that night at the arena.

Pushing down a surge of jealousy, he drifted slowly over to the telephones, picked one as close to the man as he dared and pretended to use it. He kept his back to him and his head below the partitions dividing them, just able to make out what the man was saying.

"That's right. Miles Delaney. Yes, you could describe this as an emergency. Thank you."

Simon heard him hang up. The man's name meant nothing to him. As he puzzled over their relationship, he heard Jessie's voice and wedged himself even tighter into the telephone kiosk.

"All set," she said.

"I told them this was an emergency. He should—" The phone rang.

"That was quick!"

"He's a good man," Miles informed her. He picked up the receiver before it had a chance to ring a second time. "Hello? Yes. Where? What the . . . Okay, hang on there, we'll join you as soon as we can. Good work, Jerry." Miles hung up.

"Where is he?"

Simon wanted to know too. He risked raising his head a little so he could hear better.

"Disneyland of all places. Hit men after him and where does Paul Taylor go? Disneyland!"

"Well, there are a lot of people there, I suppose, even at night and this time of year. Safety in numbers and all that," Jessie said.

"Until they close, which will be very soon," Miles said, looking at his watch. "Assuming Jerry may not have been the only one on Paul's tail, all they have to do is wait in the lot and pick him up as he leaves. For that matter, the place is like a maze. They could pick him up—or pick him *off* —almost anywhere."

"You're right," Jessie agreed. "I think Paul has made another wrong move. Let's go."

Simon waited for a moment, then popped his

head up and watched them leave. He was smiling. *You're wrong, Jessie,* he thought. *Paul may have made the best move he's made in years.* He grabbed his bag and headed for the terminal exit.

CHAPTER NINE

Disneyland at night was everything it was cracked up to be, Jessie decided. At the moment, however, she was more concerned with the size of the place than its magical ambiance. Miles and she were headed toward the entrance to the *Vieux Carré* of New Orleans, where they were supposed to meet Paul's shadow, Jerry.

"Have you ever been here before?" Miles asked as they strode purposefully through the crowd.

"Yes," Jessie replied. "When I was very small."

"Did your mother and father bring you?"

"Just my mother. My father was on a business trip. He was always on a business trip," she said without bitterness.

Jessie rarely discussed her parents, particularly her father. Miles knew he had been a workaholic, the head of a crisis management team for a large multinational corporation. He had made

157

a lot of money, had lots of contacts worldwide that still proved useful to his daughter, and had suffered a fatal coronary at a relatively young age. Miles also knew he hadn't much time for his family, but if Jessie felt badly about his lack of attention she never showed it.

"That's too bad," Miles commented. "You work hard, but at least you take time to play." He grinned at her as they walked along. "Occasionally."

Jessie knew that was a reference to the few hours she had spent with Simon, time she hadn't explained to Miles. He knew anyway and had already commented on her glow, as he called it.

"I'll have you know I am at this very moment fighting the urge to stand in line for one of these rides," she informed him. "But my father's work *was* his play. He enjoyed his life. He just pushed too hard, that's all."

"Takes all kinds of people to fill the freeways, I suppose."

"That it does," Jessie agreed. "Dad enjoyed making money, my mother enjoys spending it. It was a perfect match."

"Ah, yes. Angela McMillan," Miles repeated, smiling at the memory. "I haven't seen her since . . . well, since I became persona non grata in Rio. How is she, by the way?"

"Just fine. Hanging around the south of

France this time of year, I believe. You know how hard she is to pin down."

At last they arrived at their destination. The sounds, smells, and architecture around her made it hard for Jessie to believe she wasn't really in New Orleans. Tight little alleyways, ornate balustrades fashioned of wrought iron, fountains and courtyards and lush green foliage reminded her of the French Quarter there. A group of musicians were playing Dixieland jazz under a brightly lit candy-stripe awning, and the complex scents of Creole and Cajun cooking filled the night air.

"Psst!"

Jessie turned and saw a man waving at them. She looked at Miles. "Jerry, I presume?"

"That's him," Miles replied.

They walked over to where Jerry stood, partially concealed in the shadows of an alleyway. Where Miles was lean, Jerry could only be described as thin, almost gaunt, and quite a bit shorter than Jessie. His entire person seemed charged with nervousness, and his expression was forlorn.

"Boy, am I glad to see you two," he said as they joined him. "I tracked him here, to this place," he said, indicating a quaint restaurant across the street. "He's still in there, but they'll be closing soon. The crowd gets heavy when they start sweeping everyone toward the exit, and I was worried I might lose him."

"Jessie," Miles said, "this is Jerry."

"Glad to meet you, Jerry."

"He's very good at shadowing people, but his temperament leaves something to be desired." Miles put his hand on the other man's shoulder in a comforting gesture. "Calm down and give us the layout."

"Okay. You can see both doors from here," he said, pointing first to the front of the restaurant and then to an alcove in an alley on their left.

Miles spoke up. "Any other way out?"

Jerry shrugged. "Not one he can use. There are maintenance passageways and such, but the public can't even get close to 'em. One of the rides goes right through the middle of the place, but too fast to jump onto—you'd get squished if you tried. That's if you could get over the wall without someone stopping you, which you couldn't. They watch for things like that too."

"Okay. Now, have you noticed anyone else hanging around?" Miles asked. "Anyone who might have been doing the same thing you were?"

Jerry looked startled. "You mean another tail?" He shook his head emphatically. "If there is, they're better than I am, and that'd take some doing."

Jessie looked at Miles, arched her eyebrows,

160

then turned back to Jerry. "The people we're thinking of would be very, very good. If they are around, we have no right to keep you here any longer, Jerry."

His eyes widened. "Oh." He swallowed noisily but lifted his chin in determination. "I'll stick."

"Thank you." Jessie smiled at him. "I want you to go to the entrance to the park. Stay there and keep looking for Paul. If he comes your way, tail him. Keep an eye out for us as well. If something happens and we lose him, and we don't see you when the place closes, we'll get in touch with you via your beeper. Got it?"

"Got it," he answered, and took off, looking very happy to be leaving.

Jessie turned to Miles. "Go see if you can still get a table at that sidewalk cafe over there. You can see the back door from there," she told him. "And Miles, if our two mystery guests should show up, stay out of their way," she added in a warning tone. "Understood?"

Miles smiled enigmatically. "For the most part."

"I mean it, Miles. Now I'm going in and see what I can see. If we get separated, meet me at the park entrance."

Simon was standing in a vast maintenance room, trading insults with a man roughly his height and build but who was obviously no longer serious about keeping in shape.

"So this is what happens to old champions when they can't cut the mustard any more," he said, poking the man in the belly with his finger. "You'd be a heavyweight now, Eddie."

"I saw your last fight," the man returned, folding his big arms across his chest. "You looked like a sick carp."

"Always nice to hear from my fans."

They glared at each other for a moment, then both men broke into good-natured grins. Simon looked around at the electronic paraphernalia lining the walls. There were row upon row of drawers and shelves holding every conceivable sort of light bulb.

"It must take a lot of these to keep a place of this size operating," Simon observed.

"We change them constantly, on a rotating schedule. Can't have a burned-out bulb in the land of tomorrow."

"I suppose not." His expression turned serious. "Listen, Eddie. I need a favor."

"When have you not?" Eddie joked. He saw the look on Simon's face and stopped smiling. "What's up?"

"It's Paul. He's here, probably hiding in the French Quarter. There are some people after him."

"What has that idiot gotten himself into now?"

"I think it would be better if you don't know," Simon replied.

"Why the New Orleans section?" Eddie asked.

"He was out here on business awhile back, met this cook in a restaurant there. Lucinda something."

"Oh, *that* cook."

"Then she still works there?"

He patted his stomach. "She does indeed. Makes the best seafood gumbo in the world."

Simon breathed a sigh of relief. He hoped his brother was still on good terms with his lady friend. At the moment she was all that stood between him and whatever plans Jessie had for him.

"Think you could get him out of here without attracting attention?" Simon asked.

"In this maze? Child's play," Eddie assured him. "But we'll have to hurry. They'll be closing up in a few minutes, and anyone who isn't official will be swept out with the rest of the tourists."

"Even if Lucinda's hiding him?"

"She can't, not for long."

Simon felt his muscles tense. "Then let's go."

"Wait, these'll help," he said, grabbing something from a locker nearby. He grinned. "Disney-issue coveralls."

"Thanks, Eddie. I owe you one."

Laughing, he took off down one of the aisles, Simon close on his heels. "One? How about a hundred. I lost that much on that bout you had in San Francisco last year."

"But I won that fight!"

"That's right," he managed to say through another fit of laughter. "Now come on!"

Jessie had a mental image of Paul Taylor from a picture of him she had seen at Simon's house. There were several men in the restaurant when she entered, most with wives and families sitting beside them, and none of them bore the slightest resemblance to Paul. In fact, he was nowhere to be seen.

A young woman with curly black hair approached her. "I'm sorry, ma'am," she said. "But we're closing now."

"Oh, I was just looking for someone. I thought he came in here," Jessie said apologetically. "Did you see him by any chance? Early forties, blond hair going to gray, about five ten?"

"No, ma'am. Perhaps you'll find him at the park entrance. Everyone will be heading that way now," she replied, subtly leading Jessie toward the front door. "Good night. Come see us tomorrow."

164

Before she knew it Jessie was back outside, and indeed she soon found herself in a crowd of people being herded gently down the street. She stepped aside and Miles touched her on the shoulder.

"Anything?" he asked.

"No," Jessie answered with a frown. "I could swear the woman I talked to in there knew something, though. How about you?"

He shook his head, just as puzzled and disgusted. "No. Everyone's leaving. The only time that back door opened was to let some technicians in. No one came out."

"Technicians?"

"Two guys in coveralls. Must be some machinery to attend to in there."

Jessie looked at him, her eyebrows raised. "You don't suppose . . ."

"Another exit in the kitchen?"

"That's why he came here. He's got a friend on the inside. Come on!"

They slipped through the crowd to the back door of the restaurant, opened it, and stepped into a clean and well-kept storage room. To their left a big steel door labeled NO ADMITTANCE was swinging shut. Miles put his foot in the open space to prevent it closing all the way, then grabbed the handle with both hands and pulled.

A man dressed in coveralls poked his head out.

"What the—"

"Simon!" Jessie exclaimed.

He smiled. "Hi, Jessie. Fancy meeting you here." He slipped his elbow around the door and tapped Miles in the solar plexus, a seemingly gentle movement that had Miles gasping for air immediately. "Well, I'd like to chat, but you know how it is," Simon said airily. "Places to go, people to see. Bye!"

Before Jessie could stop him he pulled the door shut with a click. Jessie tried to open it again, but it was securely latched. "Damn you, Simon! Open this door!"

Miles was slowly recovering. "I'll kill him! I swear, the next time we meet . . ."

"You again?" the curly-haired brunette said when she came to see what the commotion was all about.

"Please, there's someone in trouble," Jessie told her. "Do you have a key—"

She had her hands on her hips and was glaring at the pair who had invaded her restaurant. "There's someone in trouble all right. You!" She turned and yelled to someone in the dining room. "Carl!"

"What?" a deep voice called back.

"Call security."

"There's no need for that," Jessie told her. Pushing Miles ahead of her, they went back out the way they had come. "We're going. See?"

A man came into the kitchen just in time to see them leave. "What was that all about?" he asked. "Call security? I *am* security, remember, Lucinda?"

"Forget it, Carl. It's too late now." She smiled. "They got away."

Late at night, after the last visitor had left, Disneyland came alive once more. An army of people descended upon the quiet streets, repairing, replacing, cleaning everything in sight, making ready for the magic to begin again the next day.

Miles and Jessie watched as long as the guards at the gate would let them. With Jerry nowhere to be found, there was some hope he had seen Simon and Paul leave and had followed them. Or he may have just gotten nervous and gone home. Jessie was so mad she couldn't see straight. Once again Paul had been within her grasp and had gotten away.

"I can't believe this," Miles remarked. "They actually steam clean the streets."

"Cleanest city in the world," the guard acknowledged. "And it will still be here tomorrow. So if you don't mind?"

They trudged to their car, a long way out in the nearly abandoned lot. Jessie was sullen and silent.

"What now?" he asked softly.

"We get in touch with Jerry," Jessie replied. "At least Paul's in good hands for the time being, so that's one thing we don't have to worry about."

"All we have to worry about is finding them."

A tremor shook her, part anger, part frustration. "You won't have to worry about getting even with Simon when we do. *I'll* strangle him for you."

Miles chuckled wryly. "He learns fast, I'll give him that. How do you suppose he got here so quickly?"

"Who knows?" she replied with an angry shrug. "I'll ask him first and then I'll strangle him."

"Getting a little too emotionally involved with your work, aren't you? This is a job, not a vendetta," he pointed out.

She thought of the smug, self-satisfied expression on Simon's face just before that door had clicked shut. "It's both, Miles. It's both."

Why hadn't Simon trusted her? If he knew where Paul was going, why hadn't he told her? She felt used and abused. Obviously the moment of intimate ecstasy they had shared hadn't meant as much to him as it had to her.

Miles opened the car door for her and she got in, completely preoccupied with thoughts of avenging her wounded pride. Though it was still a cool evening, the car seemed hot, and Jessie rolled down her window. The breeze felt marvelous on her face.

Then something pressed against her neck that was far from marvelous. "Miles . . ." she said as he slipped into the car beside her.

"I know," he replied, his throat constricted. "We have company."

"Not a word, not a sound," a gruff voice commanded from the backseat. "The guards at the gate won't come out here unless you make them, and you don't want to do that. They have families to think of."

Despite their warning, Jessie tried to speak. "What—"

The cold steel of a gun barrel pressed into her skin with renewed force. "What we are going to do is go for a little ride. To a pay phone. You were going to do that anyway, to get in touch with that little weasel of yours, right? Now you have company."

Miles gave it a try. "We don't even know—"

Jessie heard him suppress a yelp of pain, letting her know that someone had him in the same uncomfortable position. Two of them, then, hiding in the car, and she hadn't even bothered to check the backseat. Her fists clenched at her sides.

"Come now, Miss McMillan, Mr. Delaney. We all know why we're here, who we're after. Just be quiet, do as we say, and maybe you'll live through this."

The other one spoke for the first time, obviously a man of few words. But he got his point across. "Drive," he said in a gravelly voice.

Miles started the car and drove. He could see the two men in the rearview mirror. The fact that he could see their faces didn't seem to concern them at all. That worried Miles.

They were hard men, well muscled and calm, with the kind of nondescript clothing and features witnesses could never remember clearly. Their guns were steady in their hands, their expressions impassive, as if they were on nothing more than a Sunday drive in the country.

Miles didn't know them, but he knew men like them. They would be completely single-minded in their purpose, and that purpose was to catch Paul Taylor. If they did, he wouldn't see another sunrise. Anyone they caught trying to help him would very probably end up in the same condition. Miles thought of himself, and of Jessie, and could feel perspiration form on his upper lip despite the cool breeze from his open window.

"There's a phone booth," he said quietly.

"Too much light. I'll tell you when."

They drove on for a while. Every muscle in Jessie's body felt hard with tension. What if Jerry had simply gone home? Worse yet, what if he didn't answer his beeper?

She couldn't be silent any longer. "Maybe our friend doesn't know where Paul has gone."

"He'll know," the talkative one replied. "He's good. Not as good as we are, but good."

"Why didn't you just follow him, then?"

"Be quiet, lady," gravel voice told her.

The other one chuckled mirthlessly. "Because we wanted everyone together. Paul, his brother, you two. One big happy family. We're getting bored with the lot of you."

"Right there," his partner said. "That convenience store on the left."

"How nice. Some kind soul has broken out the street light. Pull to the side of the building, Delaney."

Miles did as instructed, stopped the engine, and waited. "Now what?"

"Go make your call."

"I have to call his paging service first. Then he'll call me back."

"Fine. Speak loud enough for us to hear. We'll just sit and keep Miss McMillan company."

Miles looked at her. She nodded. He got out of the car and made the call, then waited minutes that seemed like hours until the pay phone rang. He picked up the receiver.

"Jerry?" he said loudly. "This is Miles." He

listened intently for a moment. "Okay. Very good work."

"Ask him if they've settled in for the night," one of the men instructed.

Miles did, then cupped his hand over the phone. "Yes."

"Okay. Tell him to go home."

"Jerry? Thanks. You can go on home now. It was nice working with you again," Miles said, then hung up. He got back into the car.

"Don't look so surprised, Delaney. That was just to show you we're not all bad. That's the trouble with the world these days. No trust."

Jessie uttered a curt, derisive laugh. "You just don't want him hanging around. Probably didn't bring enough bullets."

"Truth is, lady," the other one ground out, "there isn't enough room in the trunk for all of you." He laughed coarsely. "Now take us to your friend, Paul Taylor."

CHAPTER TEN

It was a quiet street in a quiet neighborhood. Jessie and Miles were quiet too. They had little choice in the matter, since it was hard to make much noise with adhesive tape plastered over their mouths. Tape had been wrapped around their arms and legs as well, and did a very efficient job of keeping them in the backseat of the car where the two men had dumped them.

Miles had once bragged he could get out of any pair of handcuffs, undo any knot, but he had met his match in this expertly applied tape. He could barely move, let alone escape, though he exhausted himself trying. Perspiring freely, he sat beside Jessie in the dark, building up his strength for another attempt.

There was little Jessie could do except wait in horrified silence for the men to return. Evidently it was their intention to truss everyone up like prize turkeys, drive to some deserted place, and finish the job. At least that had been the drift of the conversation between them as they were tying Jessie and Miles up.

Something had gone wrong. She couldn't completely trust her senses, distorted as they were by fear, but it seemed a long time since the men had gone up to the house and disappeared into the shadows. As she waited her fear grew.

Simon would almost certainly put up a fight; it was in his nature, and he was protecting more than Paul's papers now. The only hope she had was that this pair seemed cocky, and perhaps they would get careless. If not, would this be the last time she would see Simon, with him unconscious—or worse?

Then the waiting ended. She nudged Miles and they watched two dark shapes come down the driveway. Each of them was dragging another dark shape behind like a big bag of potatoes. They dropped their loads unceremoniously on the ground beside the car and opened the door on Jessie's side.

A man peered into the dark interior of the car. "What in heaven's name!" He straightened and spoke to his companion. "Looks like we'll have to put them in the trunk, Paul. The backseat is already taken."

"Mmph!"

"Hold on." He stripped the tape from Jessie's mouth.

"Ouch! Simon Taylor, I was so worried about

you! They were going to dump us in the ocean. What happened in there?" Jessie was speaking so fast she had to stop and take a breath.

"Ssh!" Paul cautioned, looking up and down the deserted street. "The last thing we need now is company."

Simon laughed. "Yeah. I probably should have left the tape on her mouth. She'd be much less trouble that way."

"This the one you told me about?" Paul asked, bending down to look at Jessie's face. "Whoa. Nice." He elbowed his brother in the ribs. "Hi, Jessie. I hear you've been looking for me."

Her eyes narrowing, Jessie started to yell at them. "You could have been killed! We all could have—"

Simon cut her off by placing his mouth over hers and kissing her soundly. "Oh, shut up," he said softly when their lips parted. "Now is not the time. We've got to do something with these two goons."

"Why not just leave them here?" Jessie asked. Her head was spinning from the unexpected kiss. As relief poured over her, she found the long minutes of terror she had just endured had left her drained and confused.

"I think we've already taken advantage of Lucinda's hospitality. Leaving two unconscious and slightly damaged thugs in her living room doesn't seem like the way to repay her."

175

"Uh, excuse me," Paul interjected. "I don't want to break up this happy reunion, but we ought to get this pair into the trunk before a cop comes along."

"Or before they wake up," Simon agreed.

As they struggled with their burdens, Jessie looked at Miles. Though glad to be rescued, he didn't quite share her happiness at the moment.

"Mmph!"

"Oh, Miles. I'm sorry." She poked her head out of the open car door. "Do you think one of you could finish untying us?" she requested softly.

Simon slammed the trunk shut and walked around to the other side of the car, opened the door, and yanked the tape off of Miles's mouth.

Miles stifled a scream. "You enjoyed that, you dirty—"

"Now, Miles, be grateful," Jessie told him. Simon had a lot to answer for, but it would have to wait.

"I think I'll leave him tied up," Simon said vindictively.

Miles struggled against his bonds. "I owe you, buster."

"Yeah?" Simon shot back. "Who's the guy saving your bacon, buddy?"

"Our bacon wouldn't need to be saved if you had cooperated with us. Bloody amateur! You could've gotten us all killed!"

"You don't look too professional at the moment, hotshot," Simon returned sarcastically. He leaned over, his face inches from Miles's. "How about I wake one of those guys up and see how well you do, smart—"

"Gentlemen!" Jessie interrupted vehemently. "Please. The argument can wait." She smiled. There was more to this fight than conflicting personalities. Simon was actually jealous of Miles! "Right now, let's get the heck out of here."

"Amen," Paul agreed.

The two men glared at each other warily. At last Simon shrugged and cut Miles loose, then Jessie. They rubbed circulation back into their limbs, then everybody piled into the car, with Simon at the wheel and Jessie beside him.

Miles's stormy scowl slowly faded. Reluctantly he extended his hand over the backseat. "I don't know how you did it, but thanks."

Simon tried not to wince when they shook hands. He cleared his throat. "Some grip you've got there."

"Stop showing off, Miles," Jessie said.

"How did you develop that kind of strength in your fingers?" Simon asked as he pulled the car away from the curb.

"Pull-ups."

"Pull-ups?"

"Yeah. You grab a window ledge and pull

yourself up. Do that over and over, ten or fifteen floors a night for several years, your fingers get pretty strong."

Simon frowned. "I don't understand. Window ledges? You mean floors of a building?"

Jessie looked at the grin on Miles's face and broke out laughing. She put her hand on Simon's thigh. It was good to be alive.

"It says here," Jessie remarked as she scrutinized a copy of the Dallas *Times Herald,* "that two men were found in the parking lot of a police station in California. Bound, gagged, with multiple contusions and mild concussions, the pair had evidently been deposited there around midnight Saturday." She pushed her sunglasses up on her forehead and looked over the edge of the paper at Simon.

"Multiple contusions? What did you think you were doing, practicing for your next tournament?"

"Can I help it if I have fast hands?" he said lazily.

Jessie was sitting at the poolside table, a terrycloth robe wrapped around her. Simon was stretched out on a towel on the concrete deck, wearing only his swimsuit. She watched as he turned onto his side, fascinated by the interplay of muscles beneath his bronzed skin. Shielding his eyes from the bright sun, he leaned on one

178

elbow and took a long drink of iced tea. His gaze lingered on her smooth, uncovered legs.

"I don't care if you did take them by surprise," she said, feeling herself grow warm from more than the sunlight. "Those guys were hard cases. You should've just knocked them out and been done with it."

Simon chuckled. "It wasn't quite that easy. Do you want a blow by blow?"

"Some other time," Jessie replied, shivering even under the hot sun. It was all too real right now. Though Simon was treating it lightly, it had been a close call. She could see it in his eyes, could tell it hadn't been a one-sided brawl by the bruises he sported on his chest and back.

She turned her gaze back to the newspaper and continued. "Found by one Sergeant Williams as he was coming on duty, the two men told the bizarre tale of being mugged by a street gang."

"That's gratitude for you," Simon interjected. "I take them out of that stuffy trunk and what do they call me? A street gang."

"However, upon checking police files, the pair were identified as notorious criminals, wanted in seven states for various acts of robbery and aggravated assault, and are presently being questioned in connection with an as-yet unsolved murder in Chicago. Authorities there say they are confident of a conviction."

179

Jessie put the paper down and stood up, walking over to where Simon reclined near the pool's edge. She looked at him, at his closed eyes and peaceful expression, feeling a longing stir within her.

Kneeling beside him and kissing his forehead, she asked, "How does it feel to bring two public enemies to justice?"

"Except for the sore ribs, pretty good," he replied. He pulled her down to sit beside him. "But you ought to know how it feels. In your occupation, you bring people to justice quite often, don't you?"

Jessie frowned, hearing an undertone of accusation in his voice. "Not often. Just sometimes. I'm a locator, an information finder. The people I work for—"

"Do the dirty work?" he interrupted.

Jessie stiffened, almost got up, but stopped herself. This wasn't simply idle curiosity. He was worried about Paul. So was she. Technically she had fulfilled the assignment given her by Harrold Stone. Paul was in Simon's guest room fast asleep, exhausted from the almost constant running he'd been doing for the last few weeks. Once he had rested, she was supposed to take him back to New York.

But would Simon let her? Would she even try? Truthfully, she had been putting off that decision, though it had plagued her all the way back

180

from California. Her sleep last night had been fitful because of it—not that she and Simon had gotten much sleep in any case.

The excitement of their narrow escape from the two thugs had worked a magic on them, and they had spent a night of torrid passion in each other's arms. Just thinking of last night brought a tingle of delight to her spine. But Simon was looking at her expectantly, and she knew she would have to answer.

"The various people who hire me decide what is to be done with whomever or whatever I find," she said at last, reminding herself as well as him. "I'm usually picked for the job in the first place because they don't want the authorities involved. They trust me to work quietly, in confidence, and to get results."

Simon looked at her, his eyes hard. "That's why I took matters into my own hands. *Someone* has to look out for Paul. You're not. You do your part and wash your hands of the rest."

"Simon . . ."

"Right?" he demanded.

"Not this time," Jessie replied quietly.

She was supposed to take Paul back, that was her job. But her feelings of duty held little power against the emotions boiling inside her. She really didn't have a decision to make. It had been made for her, the first time they had made love, perhaps the first time Simon had kissed her, right here by this pool.

"What's so special about this time?" Simon asked.

Jessie lowered her eyes. "This time I care about what happens after I've done my job," she answered softly. "Paul is in trouble, neither of us can deny that, but I want to do whatever I can to minimize that trouble."

"Why?"

She looked up, met his questioning gaze, reached out to touch the strong line of his jaw. "I don't want either of you hurt, not if I can help it. I care about your brother, because I care about you, Simon."

"Jessie." He pulled her into his arms, possessively covered her mouth with his. Their lips melted together, need flowing between them through the touch of their tongues. "I'm sorry," he murmured against the softness of her throat. "When you took off in Denver, I was so mad, I wanted to strangle you."

She cradled his head, pressed him to her breasts, desire filling her being with liquid fire. "I had much the same thing in mind for you when I saw you in that restaurant."

"I don't know which worried me more, the thought of Paul in jail, or the possibility I would never see you again."

"I thought you'd get yourself killed," Jessie said, her voice little more than a husky whisper.

"I had the same fear for you."

She couldn't bear to think about how close they had both come to that fate. The problems they faced were far from over, but time was so precious, and they had wasted too much of it already on fears and doubts.

"Simon, I want you," she said urgently. "Now."

His hands roved over her beneath her robe, bringing her body alive. "I want you too, Jessie. I think I've wanted you every minute of the day since we first met." He stood up, scooping her into his arms, inhaling her fragrance and feeling desire race through his every fiber.

Warmed by the sun, his skin felt hot to the touch as she dug her fingers into the muscles of his broad back. He carried her into the coolness of the house, down the hall to his bedroom. The sheets felt icy and delicious against her skin as he reverently undressed her, his own brief suit joining hers on the floor. Then their bodies touched and flames leapt within her again.

Beside him, Jessie lay stretching her supple body, sleek as a cat. Arching her back, arms reaching over her head in invitation, she enticed him, her breasts undulating in gentle response. Her hips joined the sensual flow as well until each part of her body seemed to be reaching out to him, teasing his desire for her to the surface.

Eyes closed, Jessie could hear Simon's reaction to her. The soft, hoarse rasp of his breath coming quicker, music to her ears. Through half-lidded eyes she studied his body. She knew every angle and plane; every ripple in his strong body had been intimately etched into her memory. She wanted to relive that memory again and again, wanted to feel him inside her, his heated flesh against hers, moving in time.

"Simon, yes!" she cried out, inching closer and closer to him until their bodies melded as one. His desire was strong, powerful, and hard, a masculinity that would have blown her like a leaf before a hurricane had not her own passionate femininity been just as strong. They were ideally matched, taut and athletic, giving and taking with equal joy. Fitting together, striving together, they reached an ecstatic peak, gasping for breath in a damp tangle of sheets, only to recover and begin again.

Simon's fingertips softly traced her lovely face. Her deep-green eyes, shaded by arching eyebrows, were capable of expressing a multitude of emotions. Right now they were looking up at him, passion-filled. As he followed the curve of her mouth, her tongue darted out to wet her love-parched lips and touch his hand.

Jessie drew Simon's face closer, her fingers

threading his thick hair as their lips met. Gently, almost hesitantly they kissed, whispery petal-soft kisses growing more urgent as their desire began anew. Gasping for breath, she lay back on the pillow.

Simon left a trail of butterfly-light kisses down her creamy throat before lowering his mouth to her breasts. He could feel the increasing beat of her heart as he lingered there, tracing the already taut nipples, gently nibbling with his teeth. His mouth closed over one and then the other, her uneven breathing catching as he continued to stroke her boldly.

Jessie's nimble hands could not stay still, continuing to caress him, running up and down his back, grasping firm buttocks before sliding down over his sides and back up to his broad chest, teasing his nipples. Stroking them with her tongue, she enjoyed the feeling of softness turning hard beneath her mouth.

Slowly, leisurely, with moist kisses and gentle hands, they made love to each other. Closer and closer to the flames they danced, and again and again they held back, until together they erupted into a fiery blaze of passion that engulfed them in its heated grasp.

When finally satiated, they held each other, deeply moved by what they had shared yet laughing softly, almost shyly, at themselves and their wild abandon.

"I hope your brother is a sound sleeper," Jessie said quietly as she drew lazy circles on his chest with her fingertips.

"He is. Listen."

She did, and heard Paul's snores even through the thick walls and locked door. She laughed. "Good. I was prepared to be embarrassed."

"So was I." He kissed the top of her head. "I'm glad Miles is out. I think he resents my affection for you."

Affection? The word seemed too lighthearted to her. What she had for Simon was love, pure and glorious. Still, it had taken her long enough to come to that conclusion, even longer to admit it to herself. Such a realization took time, and she was too happy with what they had right now to demand more from him. And she was well aware it took more than love to make a relationship work. Love was one thing, commitment another thing entirely.

She loved Simon, but her past, her life itself was so much different from his. Love was not a cure-all; no matter how happy they were together, it still might not work out between them. How could she ask for commitment when she wasn't even sure she could make one herself?

Her thoughts returned to Simon's assessment of Miles. She knew he wondered about their relationship. So had she at times over the years.

It wasn't easy to describe, even harder to categorize. Miles had been a friend, a mentor even. Though he had shown real jealousy in the past, and she had certainly enjoyed that attention, they had both cherished their friendship too much to risk anything deeper. He really wasn't her type, and what was more, she wasn't his.

"Miles really isn't as much the jealous type as he is protective," Jessie explained. "He's my guardian angel. And my friend."

"I see. He resents me because he thinks I'm going to take his place," Simon said thoughtfully.

Jessie shrugged. "I guess."

"Well, then, he shouldn't worry."

She tilted her head to look at him. He was giving her a look that made her feel good all over. "Oh?"

"Because I have no intention of being your friend. Or at least not *just* your friend," he explained, his voice deep and sensual. "Besides, I get the feeling Miles has, um, a certain kind of experience I'm in no position to replace," he added, his expression one of puzzlement.

Jessie smiled secretively. "True."

"How long have you known him?"

"Quite awhile."

"How did you meet?"

She chuckled and propped herself up on her elbow, gazing at him mischievously. "I get this feeling you're pumping me for information. Why don't you just come right out with it?" she asked, her eyes sparkling with amusement.

"Okay. This story about you, the one that's all over the underground. Is that just something you started to cover up your real occupation, or is there more to it than that?"

"More?" she asked innocently.

Simon leaned over and gently nipped her nose. "Next time I'll bite it off. Now tell me the truth."

"I knew it," she said dramatically. "You think my nose is too big."

"You little witch!" He started to tickle her.

"Stop! Stop!" When he did, she lay back on the bed and sighed. "All right. The fact that some people—especially other thieves of various sorts —think I'm a semiretired thief gives me a certain edge, a certain amount of information I wouldn't otherwise have access to," she explained. "So I encourage the story, even spread it around. But," she added, looking candidly at him, "I didn't start it. Not really. I mean, I suppose I did in a way—"

"Stop waffling," he warned. "I said the truth."

"Waffling?" She started to sit up. "That reminds me, I'm hungry."

Simon pushed her back down. "Later."

Jessie took a deep breath, let it out, and continued. "My father was a sort of troubleshooter

188

for a large, multinational company. He made a lot of money, traveled all over the world. My mother and I traveled with him."

"You speak of him in the past tense."

She nodded. "Yes. He's gone, of a heart attack. The money's still around, or most of it. My mother spends it quite freely, but then again, with the amount he left and the provisions he made to continue its growth, she can afford to," Jessie said. "Anyway, we lived all over. I was born in America, spent a lot of my childhood in Europe. I speak a couple of languages fluently and can get by in a few others. I've hobnobbed with the rich and famous, played with the jet set, wintered in Rio, and summered in Switzerland."

"A well-rounded education," Simon remarked, looking at her with a new appreciation. "Now get to the good part."

Jessie laughed. "Okay. Most people find this hard to believe, but that kind of life can get rather boring."

"Sure. All that fun and sun," Simon remarked dryly. "My heart goes out to you, you poor darling."

"It's true," she said, punching him on the arm playfully. "Vacations are fun because you can look forward to them, and because you have your work to compare them to."

Simon shrugged doubtfully. "Moderation in all things, I suppose."

"Right," Jessie replied. "Anyway, some of the crowd I hung around with turned to high risk sports, gambling, things like that. I, on the other hand, got involved in something else."

"Crime?"

"Do you want to hear this or not?"

Simon chuckled, running his fingers through her hair in a soothing gesture. "Sorry. I'm all ears."

"My mother was very much a part of the social scene. Still is," Jessie continued. "I can tap into a wide range of information there, as well, but that's another story. As a part of that scene, she had many friends, and they had enough jewelry between them to start their own diamond cartel."

"The plot thickens," Simon said, raising his eyebrows in obvious interest. "Go on."

"I happened on a lovely idea one night. Why not pretend to be an international jewel thief? I would pick someone out of the crowd at a party or other social function, and plot ways to relieve them of their jewelry. Danger, intrigue, intricate plans carried out in the dead of night, that sort of thing really stirred my imagination."

Simon was amazed. "You're kidding?"

"No," she replied, shaking her head in wry amusement at the memory. "Thinking back on it, it was a bizarre way to amuse myself, but for me it was more exciting than jumping out of an airplane or taking up hang gliding."

"If it was all pretend, how did you get your reputation in the underground as a thief?" Simon asked, suddenly alarmed. "You never actually stole anything, did you?"

Jessie laughed at his shocked expression. "No. I would follow my victim around, dig for information, make what I considered foolproof plans, and stop just short of carrying them out," she assured him. "As I said, bizarre but relatively harmless—or so I thought. Little did I know that while I was stalking other people, somebody was stalking me."

"The cops?"

"Heavens no. It was Miles."

"Miles!" Simon exclaimed.

Jessie nodded. "He *was* a jewel thief, one who was at the same time a respected member of the society he stole from. He was one of the best, the cream, so to speak, and he thought I was after some goodies he had been about to acquire for himself."

"Uh-oh."

"You said it. And to top it off, he knew me, was an acquaintance of my mother's, in fact. I'll never forget the look on his face when I told him what I was up to." Jessie winced as she remembered the outrage in his voice. "He read me the riot act, shook me till my teeth rattled. Then he made very sure I understood just how dangerous a game I was really playing."

Simon frowned, confused. "Odd sort of thing to do, wasn't it? I mean, after all, who was he to preach to you? I did just hear you tell me he was a professional thief?"

"He was. Accent on professional," she replied. "He had a kind of code, no excuse for being a criminal, of course, but a fairly admirable code nonetheless. Miles stole only diamonds, and only from people who literally dripped in them."

"People insured against the loss, naturally?"

"Naturally. But like I said, that's still no excuse for committing a crime," she said with a conviction born from having thought the matter out. "Somebody pays for everything that's stolen. The insured pays his or her premiums, the insurance company reimburses them for the loss, then the little people like you and I pay a higher price for our car insurance."

Simon cocked his head and looked at her curiously. "I don't understand what Miles was worried about. You were just playing a game, and with those high morals, you hardly could've gotten into much trouble."

"That's what I thought," Jessie said with an ominous expression. "But he informed me otherwise. By messing around like I was, I might have brought attention onto him or some other real thief. And though he was letting me go with a stiff warning, there were a lot of thieves who didn't share his scruples." She paused, shivered slightly, then continued, her voice turning more serious. "He also said he didn't believe me. He took a very dim view of my little game, and told me that no matter how much I denied it, he considered me a thief who simply hadn't gotten around to stealing anything yet."

Simon shivered inwardly as well. Though fascinated with the story she was telling him, he couldn't bring himself to believe it was true. One look in her eyes, however, and he knew it was. Instead of being jealous of Miles, he now felt forever in his debt. If he hadn't stopped her . . .

"It was hardly the exciting, devil-may-care life I had envisioned," Jessie said, shaking her head at how foolish she had been. "Nevertheless, I became fascinated with how Miles went about his profession. Partly to keep an eye on me, partly to give me a fighting chance should I decide to take off on my own, he took me on as a kind of apprentice. I was involved on the periphery, learned the trade from the outside, so to speak."

"And that's where you got the reputation?"

"That's right," Jessie replied. "By association."

"But—"

"But I'm not a thief?" she completed for him. "No. Neither is Miles, not anymore. Among other things, his knees started to give out."

"Occupational hazard?"

Jessie nodded. "Cold, damp nights, a lot of stress on the tendons from climbing and creeping about. He takes better care of himself now and you can hardly tell it, but he developed arthritis in his knees."

"You said his knees were only part of the reason he quit. What happened?" Simon asked.

"One night, after a particularly tricky safe-cracking job, he was making his escape across a rooftop and one knee gave out. He fell fifteen feet, broke his arm, and passed out. When he came to, the gems he'd stolen were gone."

"Gone?"

"Vanished. The theft was reported, but the jewels never surfaced. Miles certainly didn't have them, and the only people who could handle that sort of merchandise didn't have them either," Jessie told him.

"Then who had them?" Simon wanted to know. He was completely fascinated.

Jessie arched her eyebrows, carried away by the mystery she was unfolding for him. "That's what the police wanted to know. Because of certain irregularities in the victim's finances, they suspected he still had the gems, had reported them stolen as part of an insurance scam."

"Did he?" Simon asked impatiently.

"I'm getting to that," she answered. "You must be one of those people who skips ahead and reads the ending of a book first."

"I even go to the theater early enough so I can watch the end of a movie first. Go on."

"I told you Miles was a specialist with safes. In fact, he was too good. An artist you might say. Though they weren't positive enough to arrest him, the police were fairly certain he was the one who had pulled the job."

"So they came knocking on his door . . ." Simon prompted.

"And offered him immunity from prosecution if he could help them prove their theory. With my help, he managed to recover the gems and do just that," Jessie explained. "We found out that the owner of the gems had been watching when Miles cracked his safe. Miles was lucky he fell from that rooftop, because otherwise he might have been killed. As it was, the man just watched him fall, took the gems back while Miles was unconscious, and put them in a safe place, then reported them stolen."

"Ah-ha! So that's how you got into this unusual profession of yours?"

"Right. I found I liked rooting around for information no one else could find. I brought the guy to justice, and got Miles off the hook."

"Case closed," Simon said with a satisfied grin.

"And because he had come so close to getting caught, Miles gave up theft forever."

"Not quite, I'm afraid."

Simon sighed. "Then what *did* it take to put you two back on the straight and narrow?"

"The detective handling the case was true to his word. He didn't bring charges against Miles for stealing the gems in the first place. But he told him—and me—that if he ever even heard about another safe being opened in Miles's inimitable style, he'd put us both away and lose the key."

"The end?"

Jessie laughed. "The end."

"Good." He got up and put on a shirt and a pair of jeans. "I'm hungry!"

Jessie got up as well, stretched sensuously, and wrapped her terry robe around her pleasantly exhausted body. "Me too." She looked at him, a hesitant smile tugging at the corners of her mouth. "Do you still like me? Even now that you know my wicked and shadowy past?"

"This may come as a surprise to you, sweet Jessie," Simon replied, taking her into his arms, "but I couldn't care less what you were before you met me. I wanted you from the first moment I set eyes on you. If nothing you've done so far in our crazy relationship has changed that, how could anything in your past make the slightest difference?"

She lowered her eyes from his possessive gaze. "I just thought that maybe, once the mystery was gone, or when you found out what I almost became . . ."

Simon tilted her head up and kissed her tenderly. "I almost became a common street tough," he reminded her. "We all have the right to be young and foolish." He hugged her fiercely against him. "And as far as mystery goes, if it's possible I find you even more attractive, more mysterious than ever. You're a night shadow. *My* night shadow."

"Oh, Simon." She sighed happily. They kissed again, passion rekindling within them once more. But the sound of the front door opening and closing interrupted them.

"Hey!" Miles called out. "Anybody hungry? I got pizza."

Though it obviously gave him pause to see Simon and Jessie come out of the bedroom together, he didn't seem very surprised either. And finally, as Paul joined them in the kitchen and they were all devouring the pizza he'd brought, Miles accepted the inevitable and started smiling.

He winked at the happy couple. "Have a nice afternoon?" he asked with a sly grin.

"Very pleasant," Jessie replied.

"Good," he said, and meant it.

"What have you been up to?" she asked. "Besides saving us all from starvation." She made a grab and beat Simon to the last piece of pepperoni pizza.

"Well, I arranged to have Simon's car moved to the long-term parking lot at Denver Stapleton—"

"You did?" Simon interrupted. He looked at Miles, surprised by the thoughtful gesture. "I'd almost forgotten about that. Thanks, Miles."

He shrugged. "What are friends for? Besides," he added seriously, "it was the least I could do. And it only took a call to a friend of mine who works there."

"The keys—" Simon began.

"He won't need a key."

Simon chuckled. "Oh."

"Miles can be very sweet when he wants to be, can't you, Miles?" Jessie interjected. She fed the last bite of her pizza to Simon.

"Oh, by the way, you owe me a hundred dollars," Miles told Simon.

He almost choked. "What for?"

"That's how much my friend charged for moving your car," he answered with an innocent grin. "Better than a parking ticket and a tow to the impound lot, wouldn't you agree?"

Simon pursed his lips, felt Jessie jab him in the side, and nodded. "Yeah. Thanks, Miles."

"How about our situation?" Jessie asked.

"What's the rest of the world doing while we're recuperating from our jet lag?"

"The arrest of the two thugs Paul's company sent after him seems to have flustered them a bit. They appear to be biding their time now, seeing what's going to happen."

Sullen and quiet so far, Paul finally spoke up. "If I know my good buddies," he said sarcastically, "they're digging a big hole and tossing all their records into it. As soon as they get their hands on me, they'll throw me in there too."

Jessie looked at him. He resembled Simon somewhat, around the eyes especially, and they had the same strong nose and jaw line. But Paul had the look of a man who had lived a hard, fast life and hadn't enjoyed it all that much.

It was quite a contrast to Simon's face. In his laugh lines and easy smile, it was easy to see Simon's zest for life. Paul looked tired, much older than the six years she knew were between the brothers.

"We're not going to let that happen, Paul," she told him. "But you've got to help us."

He laughed bitterly. "I knew that was coming. Who do you work for? The SEC?"

"Indirectly."

"Yeah. Doesn't everyone?"

Jessie frowned. "What's that supposed to mean?"

"You think my associates haven't bought them

off? I'll answer a few questions, enough to let them figure out what needs to be covered up where, and then I'll mysteriously disappear."

Simon turned to Jessie, his eyebrows arched. "Well?" he asked. "Is that true? More important, will you let it happen if it is?"

She had been right. The trouble and doubt between them was far from over. Whether the delicate romance they had would survive depended upon how well she did her job. She was determined to do it very well indeed.

Jessie looked him in the eye. "No. I won't," she promised. "But he has to cooperate with me."

"Cooperate!" Paul exclaimed sarcastically. "What do I have to cooperate *with?* Without those papers the Terlin brothers took from Simon, I don't have zip. It's my word against theirs. And to top it all off, *I* have to incriminate *myself* in order to tell my side of the story. Some deal!"

"No one forced you to go along as far as you did, Paul," Simon reminded him. "You knew what you were getting into."

He slumped in his chair, shaking his head in disgust. "I screwed up and I know it. But is it fair for me to go to jail while they walk?"

"It doesn't have to happen like that," Jessie said. "I don't know who your partners bought off, but they didn't buy the man who hired me."

She thought of the blustery Harrold Stone. "No one can."

"Sure," Paul said. "Tell me all about it."

"Hey, big brother," Simon said quietly. "I'm not fully convinced we can pull this thing off either, but I do know our best chance is with these two." He waved his hand at Jessie and Miles. "So you hear her out and quit complaining. *You* got yourself into this mess. I don't see a hell of a lot of other people around here trying to help you. Do you?" he demanded.

Paul lifted his head and looked at his brother. Jessie could see the trust, the love between them. She wondered how often they had helped each other out of difficult spots in the past. In her imagination she could see Paul taking the blame for something his kid brother had done, getting a whipping for it and not blinking an eye. Or Simon, explaining to an upset girl friend why Paul didn't want to see her any more. Simon had risked his life to save Paul, and though she wasn't entirely sure of Paul's character, she had the feeling he would do the same.

They were brothers. She envied the bond between them. There was more to it than the old cliche about blood being thicker than water. There was love, understanding, and unqualified acceptance. Could she forge a bond with Simon anywhere near that strong? More than anything in her life, she wanted to try.

"I'm sorry, kid," Paul said at last. "You guys saved my life. I owe you, all of you." He sighed. "To tell you the truth, I'm glad someone in authority finally caught up with me. I'm tired of running."

He ran his hands over his face, looking haggard and weary. "Those papers were my insurance policy, just to make them leave me alone. I didn't want the money, I didn't want justice, I just wanted *out*. But I swear, if I had them now, I'd use them to put those guys away even if it meant sharing a cell with them."

"Miles?" Jessie looked at him questioningly.

"I told you I'd been busy today," he answered with a smile. "I'm fairly certain the papers still exist, because that rancher who hired the Terlins to steal them has been threatening his partners with them."

"Which means he has them in his possession," Jessie said, thinking out loud. "And it shouldn't be too hard to figure out where he would stash them."

Paul sat up excitedly. "That's easy. I know who you're talking about. He has a ranch, not far from here as a matter of fact." His face fell. "But the place is like a fortress."

"Bingo," Simon interjected. "Where better to stash something than a fortress?"

"But you'd need a master thief to get into the

place and get the papers out!" Paul exclaimed. "It's hopeless!"

"Oh, I wouldn't say that," Jessie replied, looking thoughtfully at Miles.

Simon smiled broadly. "No, I wouldn't say that at all."

CHAPTER ELEVEN

"Stop looking at me like that," Miles said.

Simon was grinning like a Cheshire cat. "It just so happens, Paul, that we have a master thief in our midst."

"You told him?" Miles scowled.

Jessie shrugged and linked her arm through Simon's. "It seemed like the thing to do at the time."

"I'm retired."

"Just this once," Jessie coaxed. "It'll be fun."

Miles glared at her. "Fun? Need I remind you what happens to *both* of us if I ever get caught cracking another safe?" He crossed his arms on his chest and looked away. "I won't do it."

Paul sat watching the exchange in puzzlement. "Would somebody mind tell me what's going on?"

"Miles has a wealth of experience in, um, acquiring other people's possessions," Simon explained. "So to speak."

Paul looked at Miles thoughtfully. "Oh, yes. Pull-ups on window ledges. You're a burglar?"

"I *was* a *thief*. Not a burglar," he replied with a disdainful air.

"One of the best," Jessie said.

Miles looked at her, one eyebrow raised haughtily. "Did you say *one* of?"

She laughed, glanced at Simon, and winked. "Don't let him fool you. He's tempted, all right."

Simon saw it too. "Miles, I hardly think a man in possession of stolen documents would report it if someone stole them back."

"Especially," Jessie added, "when those documents contain incriminating evidence of his part in a stock manipulation deal. He might try to get them back again, but he wouldn't report a break-in."

Miles rubbed a hand along his jaw. "I'd need details," he said thoughtfully. "A map of the interior of the place, probable locations for a safe, security arrangements."

"No problem," Paul said. "The guy is very fond of entertaining, and a big talker. I've been to the place more than once. I can draw you a map."

"We got him," Jessie whispered in Simon's ear.

Miles barely noticed. "Maybe." He looked sharply at Paul. "Like a fortress, you said?"

"Guards. Dogs. A rather elaborate alarm system." Paul frowned uneasily. "Not to mention the Terlin brothers."

"The alarms," Miles said, speaking quickly. "Main control box?"

"Yes," Paul answered.

"Where?"

"In the master bedroom." He hesitated. "I think."

Miles looked disgusted. "You think?"

"I was at a party he threw. Met this cute . . ." He glanced at Jessie and trailed off. "Anyway, I saw this box under his bed. Rows of switches and little green lights, a place for a key. Big red button on the side."

"A panic button," Miles decided. "To activate the entire system in an emergency. There are probably other relays throughout the house, but that sounds like the main unit."

Simon had to ask. "What were you doing *under* the bed?"

"I . . . fell off," Paul replied, his face turning red.

Jessie started laughing, but sobered quickly when she saw the look on Miles's face. *He* was grinning widely now.

"I think I have the beginning of a plan," Miles said, looking at each of them in turn. He stepped over to Simon.

"Uh-oh," Simon intoned.

"Guards, dogs, the Terlin brothers," Miles

said. He patted Simon on the back. "Sounds like just the kind of physical endeavor at which you appear to excel."

Simon started to object. "But—" Then he thought of the lump on his head and of a set of tobacco-stained teeth grinning at him as he passed out. "I'm your man," he said with a grim smile.

Miles turned to Paul. "You are the only one who knows exactly what it is we're after."

Paul's eyes widened. "Simon's seen them," he blurted.

"I should think your brother might have his hands full," Miles pointed out. "Besides, I take it the documents in question are quite complex?"

He shifted uneasily in his chair. "I could explain them to you, and—"

"No," Miles interrupted. "This man probably had a copy altered to omit the evidence against him. We need the originals if they still exist. What would take me several minutes—minutes we won't have—you could tell in a glance."

Paul sagged a little, seeing the logic of his argument. "Okay. It's about time I started paying my dues anyway."

"Now. Jessie." Miles turned to her and smiled. "Seems like old times, doesn't it?"

Simon held up his hand. "Whoa. Stop right there." He took Jessie's hand and squeezed it. "She stays here," he said flatly. "It sounds like a lark right now, but this is going to be dangerous. I won't let her go and that's all there is to it."

Miles sighed, turning his eyes to the ceiling. "Oh, brother," he muttered. "Did you ever say the wrong thing."

Jessie pulled her hand away, small spots of color appearing on her cheekbones. "Let me?" she asked Simon in a tense, quiet voice. "Did you say you wouldn't *let* me go?"

Simon was startled by the fury in her eyes. "Jessie . . ."

"No one tells me what I can and can't do, Simon," she said, the muscles of her throat growing taut. *"No one."*

Her outrage was so sudden, so surprising in the face of what they had just shared and the feelings he thought were growing between them. He felt his own temper rising.

"Maybe it's time somebody did," he shot back.

"What's that supposed to mean?"

"This is all a game to you, isn't it?" Simon asked. "You're still that young girl looking for kicks. Placing yourself in danger for the thrill of it all."

Even through her anger Jessie felt the sting of his words. He was right, in a way, and she knew it. She *did* like the danger, the thrill of the chase. Her occupation fed a need for excitement that had been a part of her for as long as she could remember.

"I don't have to justify myself to you," she said. "I was hired to find your brother, to bring him to New York to answer questions. Along the way I made a promise to help him get out of this mess, and I'm going to keep that promise." Jessie glared at him. "Whether you like it or not!"

"I don't like it," Simon replied, raising his voice. "I don't like it at all! I was only thinking of your safety."

"What you're doing is trying to think *for* me," she pointed out. "If you want to help Paul, you have to let me do my job."

Miles could tell Simon was thinking about what she had said. Though hesitant to do so, he decided he had better take sides. This argument wasn't getting them anywhere.

"Jessie is a vital part of my plan, Simon," Miles told him. "Somebody has to get inside, get the key, and turn off the alarm system. And it has to be done by guile, not force. Stealing back the documents won't get us in trouble with the law, but mounting an armed attack on the place most assuredly will."

Frustrated, anger still plain on his face, Simon had to nod reluctantly. "I see what you mean," he said quietly. "But that doesn't mean I have to like it."

Jessie made a visible effort to calm her own anger. "Face facts, Simon. Paul needs those documents to present his case and save his neck. We all have to work together to get them."

Simon took a deep breath, held it for a moment, then blew it out slowly. "All right. What do you propose to do?"

"You said this rancher entertains quite a bit?" Miles asked Paul.

"A regular party animal," he replied.

"Then those papers are as good as ours."

Simon looked at Miles and Jessie. They were grinning at each other, obviously in tune with each other's thoughts. He again felt a stab of jealousy at their closeness.

Then he, too, began to see their plan take shape in his mind. The implications of it alarmed him. "Wait a minute," he said. "Just what is her part in this?"

"Think you can manage it, Jessie?" Miles asked, though he already knew the answer.

Jessie nodded. "If I can get close enough to him, I'm sure I can arrange to get an invitation to one of his parties. From there it should be a piece of cake."

"A piece of cake!" Simon stood up in agitation. "Let me get this straight. You're going to get invited to a party at this guy's ranch, get the key to the alarm system from him, somehow get into his bedroom . . ." He trailed off, his blood boiling at the very thought.

Jessie smiled innocently at him. "Something wrong?"

"And . . . and . . ." Simon spluttered. He was so frustrated he couldn't speak. His brother needed help, and this was the only way. He felt torn in two, caught between brotherly love and his desire for this beautiful, infuriatingly independent woman.

"All right, damn it!" Simon muttered. Dejected, he sat down again. "Let's iron out the details." Then he fixed Jessie with a warning gaze. "But after this is all over, you and I are going to have a serious talk about the insane way you make a living."

Jessie matched his threat with one of her own. "Yes, we'll have a talk. But it may not turn out the way you want." *I am what I am, Simon Taylor*, she thought. *And it will take more than my love for you to change that.*

Miles cleared his throat, feeling a tension between them so thick he could almost cut it. He sympathized with Simon. He had often felt the same misgivings about Jessie and her enjoyment of danger. But he also knew better than to try to change her.

"All right, people," he said in a businesslike manner, "here's what we're going to do. . . ."

It wasn't Bergdorf Goodman, but Neiman-Marcus in Dallas definitely had the same kind of ambiance. Jessie decided it was the smell of the place, that heady aroma of cold, hard cash.

Nathan Lockheart, on the other hand, was not quite what she had expected. Jessie had envisioned a near-caricature—an ultra-rich rancher in cowboy boots and Stetson hat, drawling and looking for a place to spit.

That was not the case. He was smooth, almost slippery, and the trace of Texan accent in his voice was so soft it seemed almost an affectation. His clothes were finely tailored, his manicured hands a telling sign of just how far he distanced himself from the source of his wealth. Paul had said Nate got no closer to the actual process of ranching than a weekly perusal of the books. He was a dandy, and Jessie took an instant dislike to him.

It had been an easy task to find him. Paul had also informed her that Lockheart was a compulsive shopper. A man of his means would almost surely be a frequent visitor to Neiman-Marcus. His red Porsche with the personalized license plate—NATE—wasn't hard to track. The tough part was yet to come.

Jessie had followed him into the store, pretending interest in the various displays while she watched him from behind her sunglasses. He bought a few items, various accessories from menswear. He had his favorite clerk in every department, with whom he chatted amiably.

She saw her chance when he strolled over to look through the vast selection of cologne. Perhaps it wasn't going to be as hard to get his attention as she first thought. Mr. Nathan Lockheart had quite an eye for the ladies.

"Lucky man," he said, smiling at her and showing a mouthful of too-perfect teeth.

"Excuse me?" Jessie returned with just the right amount of coolness. Interested, but hard to get.

"Lucky man," he repeated, "to have such a lovely woman shop for him." His eyes roved over her, checked her left hand for a ring. His smile broadened. "Selecting a scent for your father, perhaps?"

"Oh." She smiled too, allowed a slightly embarrassed tone into her voice. "No, it's for a—a friend. And I'm afraid I'm at a loss." Flustered. Even a little helpless.

"Perhaps I can help. What kind of man is he?"

Jessie thought of Simon. She couldn't help it. He had been sullen since their argument yesterday. "Oh," she said with a perturbed sigh, "arrogant. Pig-headed."

He laughed and winked with the air of a conspirator. "I see. Maybe you would rather I take you over to sporting goods and help you select a knife?"

Jessie hadn't giggled since she was thirteen, but she did so now. She didn't like it. It made her throat feel funny. "We had a bit of an argument, I'm afraid," she confided. "I really don't know why I'm buying him anything at all."

"A woman of your beauty should receive apologies, not give them," Lockheart said.

My sentiments exactly, Jessie thought. But she tittered again and told him, "Thank you." She smoothed her hand down her dress, a simple bone-white sheath, one she had bought last night for just this occasion. It was a size too small and tight across the bust and hips. "Thank you very much." She looked a question at him.

"Nathan. Nathan Lockheart," he supplied. "And you are?"

"Jessie." She extended her hand with studied limpness. "Pleased to meet you, Nathan."

He took her hand and kissed her fingertips. In Europe, it was a lovely and gallant gesture. From an American, especially *this* American, it was hokey and made her a little ill. But she played her role to the hilt. And giggled.

"Please," he said. "Call me Nate. All my friends do, and I sincerely hope we shall become friends."

"So do I," she replied. Just a touch of vamp. A slight arch to her brows.

"And may I call you Jess?"

"Please do." She almost gagged. She hated that nickname. But Paul had given her a quick rundown on the kind of women who attracted

214

Lockheart, and her job was to be just that so he would invite her to his house. Afterward, given the chance, she'd kick him in the . . .

"Tell me, Jess," he said, interrupting her pleasant fantasy, "this friend. You don't really want to buy him a gift, do you?"

"No. To tell you the truth, I don't know why I even walked in here. I'm on vacation, you see, and I met him at the zoo, and I really don't care if I see him again," she said, spilling over, slightly breathless. She looked at him, cocking her head to one side. "And I don't know why I'm telling you all this."

He still held her hand, and patted it now with fatherly concern. The gleam in his eyes was far from fatherly. "I'll tell you what, Jess. I'm having a party this evening, at my ranch." He lingered on the word ranch, trying to impress her. He was certainly impressed himself. "Tell me you'll come."

Though inside she was yelling in triumph, Jessie balked, suddenly shy. "Well, I don't know . . ."

"There will be lots of people there, lots of fascinating people. Since you came here for a vacation, let me show you some real Texan hospitality. Join me? Please?"

From the look he was giving her, she knew what kind of hospitality he hoped to show her. Was he really so stupid as to believe she was so stupid? Since he had so obviously bought this whole woman-in-distress garbage, she decided he was. It didn't say much for his character, but it said a great deal for her acting talent.

She smiled at him. "All right," she said, glad to be able to show a little backbone. "Let my friend go fish."

Nate grinned broadly. "Exactly." He took a pen and note pad from his inside jacket pocket and handed them to her. "If you'll give me the address of where you're staying, I'll send my car for you around seven."

"That will be fine. Thank you again."

"My pleasure, Jess." He bowed slightly, then turned and walked away.

Jessie watched him and muttered, "No, Nate. *My* pleasure." She wished she could be there to see his face when he found those papers gone, put two and two together, and figured out that she had conned him. On the other hand, perhaps she was giving him credit for more intelligence than he possessed.

"That was sickening," Simon told her as he drifted to her side.

Jessie had been so totally absorbed in her role playing she had almost forgotten Simon had insisted on coming along. She looked at him and shrugged.

"All part of the job."

"I can't believe he fell for that." He put his

hand on his hip and wiggled slightly. "Pleased to meet you, Nathan," he said, mimicking her voice.

Jessie smiled. "I found it rather unbelievable myself. But it worked. I have an invitation to this evening's shindig at his ranch."

As they walked out of the store together, Simon's expression grew more and more disturbed. Jessie was one heck of an actress. He could easily see why she was in such demand as a locator of things and people. She could charm the skin off a grape. More than that, the grape wouldn't even know it was naked.

"Why didn't you use that routine on me?" he asked suddenly when they were back in the car.

She looked at him, puzzled by the seriousness in his voice. "Would it have worked?"

"Hell, no!" he said vehemently.

"That's why I didn't use it," she said. "As a matter of fact, I didn't use anything on you, not after the first couple of minutes."

"Why not?"

His petulant mood was infectious. "I liked you too damn much, that's why!" she shot back.

Simon mulled that over for a while, weaving through midday traffic, retracing all the things they'd done and said to each other. He put his hand on her thigh.

"I'm sorry," he said.

Jessie was still fuming. "You should be. I do

217

what I have to do to get the job done. It's nothing personal."

Nothing personal. "*Whatever* it takes to get the job done?" he asked.

Jessie turned from watching the scenery whiz by and looked at him incredulously. "I think you'd better explain that question, buster!"

Simon cleared his throat. "I—I mean . . . just how far will you go to . . ."

She picked his hand up and deposited it back in his lap. "That's what I thought you meant," she said through clenched teeth.

Oh, Lord, Simon thought, *maybe I am just as stupid as that poor sucker she just vamped.* "Jessie, I'm sorry," he said quickly. "I'm just jealous, that's all. I—"

"Stop it!"

She looked at him, thin-lipped and furious, not even his admission of jealousy giving her the thrill it would have under other circumstances. Was he worried about what she may have done in the past, or did he still harbor a suspicion that all they had shared was no more to her than another role she was playing?

Simon made another stab at apologizing. "I didn't mean to imply—"

"Oh, just shut up and drive."

CHAPTER TWELVE

"Well, how do I look?" Jessie asked.

The foursome had taken a hotel room as the first step in their evening of intrigue, a room they would abandon as soon as Lockheart's car came to take Jessie to his ranch. She was standing in the middle of that room, modeling her party attire, a billowy silk pantsuit in shades of blue, soft gray, and white.

She looked elegant, especially compared to her male companions, who wore dark clothing for their duties of this night. The pantsuit was functional as well as alluring because she would be leaving the ranch a different way from the one in which she would arrive, most probably running.

"You look smashing, Jessie," Miles replied. "Simply smashing."

"Stunning," Paul said.

Simon stared at the vision of beauty standing before him, feeling tense and irritable. Jessie had barely said two words to him since his *faux pas* this afternoon. Her loveliness only added to his misery.

"Stunning," he agreed, an undercurrent of sarcasm in his voice. "You'll have old Nate eating right out of your hand."

"That's the general idea," she said dryly.

In her heart Jessie had forgiven Simon, but some stubborn part of her refused to accept his apologies. Jealous or not, he had no right to ask such a tactless question. How far would she go to get the job done indeed!

"Have you given any more thought to how you're going to get his keys from him?" Miles asked conversationally. He was fiddling with some bit of electronic hardware and didn't seem too concerned about her answer.

Simon, on the other hand, was very much concerned with that particular part of this scheme. He waited expectantly for her answer, his eyes riveted to hers.

"I'll just have to play it by ear," she replied. She knew what Simon was thinking and couldn't resist the temptation to taunt him. "I suppose I'll just have to get his pants off, won't I?"

Simon wasn't amused. "You'll have to do *what?*"

Miles and Paul were laughing. "You could always spill hot coffee on him," Miles suggested.

"Good idea. I'll give that consideration," Jessie said. "What do you think, Simon?"

He scowled, then went to stand at the window overlooking the freeway below.

Miles and Jessie exchanged a glance. He stood up and motioned to Paul. "Let's go for a walk. My knees are getting stiff sitting here."

When they had left, Jessie went to stand next to Simon, feeling guilty for teasing him. She knew how she would feel if the tables were turned. The idea of Simon spending the evening trying to charm some strange woman made her green with jealousy too.

"I accept," she said softly.

He turned and looked at her, again feeling the hypnotic power of her jade-green eyes. "Accept?"

"The apology you've been trying to make all afternoon. I accept. Miles was always jealous when I did this type of thing too, in a more brotherly way. I could laugh it off. But your accusation really hurt, Simon."

Simon's frown softened. "I am sorry. It wasn't an accusation, really, it was . . ." He trailed off, knowing excuses to be useless. "It's just that the very idea of you in the arms of another man makes me crazy."

"I understand." She put her hand on his shoulder. "If this were the other way around, and you

221

had to get a key from some svelte little rancher's daughter, I'd be ranting and raving too."

"Jessie." He pulled her into his arms and kissed her. "I think that's all I really wanted to know. You seemed to be enjoying yourself and—"

She cut him off with another quick kiss, then pulled back and looked at him seriously. "I can't deny that I enjoy the intrigue, the role playing. It's part of what I am. I wouldn't last two minutes in a normal, nine-to-five occupation," she explained. "But don't think for one moment I've forgotten that Lockheart sent the guys who whacked you on the head. That's part of why I'm doing this, really."

Simon looked surprised. "Revenge?"

"More like the need to see justice done, actually," Jessie replied. She smiled. "Despite the shadows in my past, I have a very sharp sense of what's right and wrong."

"I see." He returned her warm smile. "In that case, dump a whole pot of coffee on good old Nate for me will you?"

Jessie chuckled wickedly. "Tempting as that is, it probably won't be necessary." She hugged him, then stepped away and grinned at him. "Feel anything?" she asked.

"Lust?" he replied huskily.

She gave him a sidelong glance. "Not now, you'd ruin my makeup," she teased. "I mean did you feel me take these?" She held up her hand, his car keys dangling from one finger.

"How in—" Simon patted the pocket of his black slacks, then looked at her sternly. "You must have had a very misspent youth."

Jessie shrugged. "As you said once before, I've simply had a well-rounded education." She tossed his keys back to him, then went to check her appearance in a mirror on the hotel dresser. She touched up her lipstick. "It wouldn't do to have Nate think I've reconciled with my friend."

"Which reminds me, I overheard that crack about your friend being arrogant and pig-headed. Surely you didn't have me in mind, did you?"

"Heavens no," she said with exaggerated innocence.

A knock sounded on the door, and Simon let Paul and Miles into the room. As he was closing the door, the phone rang, and he watched lovingly as Jessie walked over to answer it. *After this is all over,* he promised himself, *we're going to do a lot more than have a serious talk.*

Jessie listened for a moment, said thank you, and hung up the phone. She arched her eyebrows and grinned. "That was the front desk. Lockheart's car is here."

Whistling a little tune, Miles picked up a small

bag and slung its strap over his shoulder. "Show-time!"

Nathan Lockheart's ranch was more of an estate, with the main house located on a sprawling, heavily wooded lot well away from the working ranch. The house itself was a massive colonial-style structure set in the middle of that lot, surrounded by green lawns and spreading pecan trees.

One hundred yards from the house, winding unobtrusively through the trees, an eight-foot chain-link fence marked the boundary of the property. The land on either side of the fence had not been cleared, so that in several spots big branches hung over. All somebody would have to do to gain entrance was climb a tree and drop over.

But Nate had seen to that oversight in security. As the driver pulled through an electrically opened gate, Jessie peered through the limousine's window and could just make out two watchful, compact shapes in the gathering evening shadows. Dobermans. She shivered inwardly, then turned her gaze forward to the house looming ahead of them down the winding drive.

Lights shone from every window, festive against the night sky, and she saw people milling about on the broad veranda. Some were better dressed than others, but it was an informal gathering, and Jessie was relieved to see she would fit right in. The last thing she wanted was to stand out in the crowd.

The driver pulled up in front and stopped. Her door opened, and there was Lockheart, looking jaunty and vaguely nautical in a blue blazer and gray slacks. He smiled, oozing hospitality.

"Jess. So good of you to come." He took her hand and helped her from the car.

"Hi, Nate," she said, bubbling. "I wouldn't have missed it." *But you're going to wish I had,* she said to herself.

He linked his arm through hers and escorted her up a short walk to the house. There were steps up to the veranda, and Jessie pretended to trip, grabbing him around the waist and leaning against him for support.

"Oops!" she said, and immediately pulled away from him. She grinned, feigning embarrassment. "Silly me."

Nate looked around, laughing self-consciously. This was a pretty thing, but clumsy as a cow. "Yes," he said brusquely. "Silly you."

Miles lowered a pair of binoculars from his eyes, shaking his head in admiration. "That's my Jessie," he whispered. He looked at Simon. "Sorry. *Our* Jessie."

Lying on their stomachs in the underbrush near the fence, the three men blended into the shadows. They all had on black pants, jackets, and knit caps. Miles had blackened their faces with burnt cork.

Simon felt like a fool, and the cap made his head itch. "I don't think anyone can claim possession of that woman," he whispered back. "What did she do?"

"Slipped on the porch."

Paul joined in the quiet conversation. "That's cause for celebration?"

"She did that so she would have an excuse to lean on Nate. To locate his keys."

"Just locate?" Simon asked.

"He might miss them if she takes them too soon, and she's waiting to give us a chance to get settled. She couldn't have known it was easier to get this far than we'd planned."

Simon fumed in the dark. "You mean she's in there right now, cuddling up to that jerk when she doesn't have to?" He started to get up.

Miles yanked him back down. "Be still. It can't be helped." He patted his distraught companion on the back. "If it makes you feel any better, the thought doesn't exactly tickle me either. But she knows what she's doing."

Simon sighed. "Sorry."

"No problem."

"I mean it," Simon said. "I've been a royal pain in the—"

Miles chuckled soundlessly. "That you have."

"I know we kind of got off on the wrong foot, you and I. I just want you to know how thankful I am to you for helping us."

"You're welcome. But to be honest, I'm not doing it for you. I'm doing it for Jessie."

"I'm sorry for that too," Simon muttered. "I know Jessie and you are . . . close. I must seem like an interloper."

Miles shrugged. "No. Like you said, nobody owns her. And I've never deluded myself. Jessie and I are friends, business partners in a way." He turned and grinned, his teeth white in the dark. "Besides, as close as you think you are to winning her, I can tell there are plenty of fireworks still to come. I'll always be around. You, on the other hand, are on the tottering brink."

Simon bristled. "What's that suppose to—"

"Ssh!"

A dog came out of the darkness and stuck its nose through the fence, sniffing noisily. It stood there for a moment, ears erect, gleaming eyes scanning the trees. With a disgusted growl it finally trotted away in search of more interesting things to do.

"Did you see those teeth?" Paul whispered uneasily.

"Why aren't they hanging around closer to

the house?" Simon wondered aloud. "Lots of nice, juicy guests on the other side of the fence over there."

"Training," Miles explained. "They've been trained to patrol the area within the fence, not outside it."

"Yeah, but inside the fence is where we're going," Paul muttered grimly.

Simon pulled a small bottle from his pocket, looking at it doubtfully. "You sure this is going to work?"

"Unless Paul was wrong about the dogs being male, those female pheromones will do the trick all right."

"They're male," Paul assured him. "Nate calls them his 'little boys.' "

"How sweet."

"What happens when they find out there isn't a female to go along with the scent?" Simon wanted to know.

"They'll be ticked off, that's what," Paul grumbled.

Miles chuckled. "Wouldn't you be? Just make sure you don't get any of that stuff on you," he warned Simon. "Or you'll be in for one heck of an amorous adventure."

Gallantry obviously wasn't good old Nate's strong point. Suppressing the urge to kick him in the shin, Jessie allowed him to parade her around, a mere ornament on his arm, his new bauble on show for the titillation of his friends. She wanted to scream, but it had to be endured. Simon, Paul, and Miles needed time to get into position, but they'd better hurry because it wouldn't be long before she tried to drown him in the punch bowl.

"There now," Nate said once they had made the rounds. He had Jessie off in a more or less quiet corner, his eyes lingering on the scooped neck of her top. "What do you think of my friends?"

"They're . . ." Ostentatious. Boorish. "They're very nice," she managed to say. The men ogled her, the women snubbed her as beneath their station. If they only knew.

But Nate didn't want a society woman. He wanted a plaything, someone to *ooh* and *aah* and be impressed. She bit her tongue and smiled. "You have a lovely home."

"Thank you. May I get you something from the bar?"

"Yes, please."

He tilted his head and grinned, like a shark eyeing its next meal. "You look like a champagne cocktail sort of girl to me."

"That would be nice." Anything, just get away from me you pretentious, oily . . . "You wouldn't be trying to get me tipsy, would you?"

He gave her a "who me?" look. "Heaven forbid!" he said, then went to get her drink.

Jessie took the opportunity to check her watch. It was time, and not a moment too soon. She mentally reviewed the map Paul had made of the interior of the house, fixing her position and planning her steps.

When Nate came back, she took her drink and sipped it, then put down the glass and asked, "Could you direct me to the little girls' room?"

"Certainly." He pointed to the wide, sweeping staircase at one end of the cavernous ballroom. "There are ten bedrooms upstairs, and each has a bath," he informed her haughtily. He stepped closer and whispered in her ear. "The master suite has a sunken tub with a Jacuzzi."

Jessie giggled. *Easy, stomach.* She briefly embraced him and whispered back, "Why, Nate, you beast!" Pushing him away playfully, she wiggled her fingers in a wave and sauntered off toward the stairs, his keys hidden in her other hand.

"There's the signal!" Miles whispered. "She's done it." He stuffed the binoculars back into his bag, stood up, and took cover behind a tree. The others did the same. "Now," he said to Simon. "And remember—"

"I know. Don't get any on me." He crept stealthily through the trees to a point away from their hiding spot, opened the bottle, and sprinkled it liberally but carefully on the ground just outside the fence.

In a matter of moments two highly excited dogs sprinted into view, sniffling the air and whining.

The other two men were already in the branches of the tree they had chosen, and when Simon started climbing it Miles dropped silently to the ground on the opposite side. He sat down immediately.

Paul and then Simon joined him. Simon frowned, concerned by the look of pain on Miles's face. "Knees?"

Alarmed, Miles put his finger to his lips, grimaced, then stood up and started hobbling toward the house. They helped him, practically carrying him in their excitement, putting him down when they reached the window to Nate's study.

Though the dogs were busy trying to dig a hole under the fence, Miles didn't waste time. He took a thin, strong knife and a small pry-bar from his bag, jamming one under the sash and using the other to deftly slip the lock on the double-hung window. He pried it open far enough for Simon to get his fingers in, then stuffed his tools back in the bag as Simon climbed inside the house. Simon helped his companions slide through, shut the window, and let out a long sigh.

"You call that fun?" he asked, keeping his voice low.

Miles was rubbing his knees and testing them for stability. "Now you see why I retired," he said, pain in his voice. "Thanks."

"The safe is over here, I think," Paul said quietly, a disembodied voice in the almost pitch-black room. "Behind a painting on the—"

They heard a soft exclamation, then a heavy thud as Paul fell flat on his face. He moaned in the darkness.

"Lord," Miles muttered. "What a comedy team we make." He reached out and touched Simon on the arm. "Go listen at the door. And for heaven's sake, use that pencil light I gave you!"

While Simon went and pressed his ear against the door, Miles used his own narrow-beam light to find Paul, still sprawled on the floor and holding his head.

"Get up, you fool!" he whispered vehemently. He helped Paul to his feet, then handed him the bag of tools. "Here. Hold this, and don't drop it."

"Right." Paul held the bag gingerly. "Do you have the explosives in here?"

Miles was running his fingers carefully around edges of the painting, feeling both for a hidden catch and a separate alarm. There was no alarm, and he found the catch. He swung the painting away from the wall on its hinges.

"I am a professional, not some heavy-handed jerk with a bottle of nitroglycerin," Miles informed him. "That's all this new generation knows how to do any more. Bash it open or blow it up."

"Save the lectures for later, professor," Simon called out softly. "There's a lot of activity out there."

"Did you lock the door?"

"There's no key."

"Then hold the knob so it won't turn," Miles instructed. "Why do you think we brought you along, champ?"

"Just get on with it." Jessie was supposed to give them fifteen minutes from the time she rejoined the party, then would slip away from Nate and knock on this door. How he longed to hear the three quick taps that was the code to let her in.

Miles fumbled in his bag for a moment and brought out a piece of electronic gadgetry. He attached part of it to the safe, the other part he put on the table underneath. Wires ran between the two. He started fiddling with the dial on the safe.

"What's that?" Paul asked curiously.

"Magnifies the sound of the tumblers. I was

betting he didn't have one of the silenced models."

"Betting!" Simon exclaimed.

"A calculated risk," Miles corrected. He was enjoying himself, and started to smile. "They're not all that common for home use."

"Oh, man. A stumblebum brother, a lady who gets her kicks picking pockets, and a safecracker who takes calculated risks." He sighed. "How did I get myself into all this?"

Watching in satisfaction as yet another tiny red light appeared on the device on the table, Miles pulled the handle and the safe slowly opened. "Voilà!"

"Bingo!" Paul added.

Simon turned in their direction for a moment, watching as Miles packed up the tools of his trade. "Haven't lost the old touch, I see," he retorted dryly.

"Your turn, Paul," Miles said, ignoring Simon's snide comment and stepping over to the window. He smiled. "I may take risks, Simon, but I never gamble. Come take a look."

Simon joined him, unable to suppress a chuckle despite his nervousness. "Industrious, weren't they?" he said, looking at the large hole the dogs had dug under the fence.

"They'll roam around for a while, then they'll come upon the trail of pheromone we laid on the way in. Actually, I hope they do find a female out there somewhere."

"Does seem like they deserve a reward for all that effort, doesn't it?"

"You were right about this too, Miles," Paul said. "He does have a copy without the evidence on him. But the originals are here as well." He held them up, grinning from ear to ear.

"Take them both," Simon said, "and shut the safe." He looked at the luminous dial on his watch. "Jessie should be here any minute."

Laughing laboriously at the fifteenth unfunny, off-color joke Nate had told in as many minutes, Jessie glanced casually at her watch. She sighed gratefully and tried to get his attention. He was so absorbed in preening for the group around them that it took him awhile to notice her.

"I'm sorry, Jess. I've been neglecting you, haven't I?" he said, though his voice held no hint of apology.

"No, not at all." She smiled, then added, "Nate, dear, is there a quiet phone I could use? I've decided I'm going to stay on in Dallas for a while and need to cancel my plane reservations." She fluttered her eyelashes coquettishly.

His eyes flashed and he grinned. "Why, of course you shall stay on! I wouldn't hear of you leaving until we've gotten to know each other better." He took her arm and started to lead her from the room. "There's a phone in my study."

"No!" she said quickly. "I mean, I wouldn't want to pull you away from your guests." She extracted her arm from his grasp. "I won't be a minute."

A frown furrowed his brow, but he capitulated. "All right. The study is down that corridor, third door on your left." He watched her hurry off, suspicion clouding his face.

Simon had his ear pressed so tightly to the study door that when Jessie knocked he jumped reflexively. He opened it quickly and ushered her in, closed it, and swept her into his arms.

"It took you long enough," he murmured against her lips.

"Nice to see you too," she said in a hushed voice. Her face was flushed with excitement. "Did you get the papers?"

"Yes, Paul has them. Did you have any trouble?"

"Not much. The Terlin brothers are the only guards on duty this evening, so it wasn't any trouble getting into Nate's bedroom and turning off the alarm to the safe."

"We can compare notes later!" Miles said impatiently. He was by the window, already helping Paul slip outside. "Let's get out of here before Lockheart starts pining for Jessie's company."

"Let me help." Simon assisted Miles through the window so he wouldn't jar his knees, then turned to Jessie. "You're next."

"You first."

"I insist."

He lifted her and poked her through the window feet first. Paul and Miles grabbed her and pulled her the rest of the way. As the trio made a dash for the fence, Simon started to crawl out himself, but two pairs of large hands clamped onto him and pulled him back into the room.

"Leaving the party so soon, Mr. Kung Fu?"

The Terlin brothers. Big and mean as ever. One of them slugged him in the stomach as he turned around, doubling him over. The other hit him behind the head with both fists before he could catch his breath. Simon went down to his knees, the room spinning alarmingly.

"Shouldn't we go help Mr. Lockheart with the other three, Mark?"

"Nah. He's got a gun, he can handle 'em." He grinned, showing stained teeth, and spit tobacco juice out the open window. "We'll wait here and have some fun with the champion."

"Yeah. He doesn't look very tricky now," Dan Terlin agreed. He pulled his foot back and started to deliver a swift kick to Simon's ribs.

But Simon was waiting. He grabbed the man's foot and helped it along, standing up and pulling him right off his feet. Dan hit the floor with a thud. In the same movement his own foot shot out in a blur, catching Mark Terlin in the stomach. He smiled as he heard him choking on his chewing tobacco.

And then Simon got mad.

Outside, lights were coming on, and questioning voices could be heard from the guests on the veranda.

"Where's Simon?"

"He was right behind me!" Jessie looked back toward the house.

The trio were gathered at the fence, underneath the overhanging tree limb. Simon was the only one who could jump high enough to reach it, the only one with strength enough to pull the others up after him.

The need for silence gone, Miles made a quick decision. "Climb the fence. Now!" He took off his jacket and slung it over the sharp edges at the top. "Go!" he told Paul.

Paul climbed awkwardly up and flipped over to the other side, landing with a crash in the underbrush. Miles sighed disgustedly and started pushing Jessie up the fence.

"But we have to help Simon!" she objected.

"Either he's in trouble we can't get him out of or he's giving us time to escape. Up you go!" He excused himself and put both hands on her shapely rear, pushing her the rest of the way over. Unlike Paul, she flipped nicely and landed on her feet in a crouching position.

"There he is!" Jessie said excitedly, pointing to a dark shape that dove through the window and came up running.

"Goody for him," Miles muttered, wincing as he climbed the fence. Unlike the other two, he had to straddle it and climb down the other side as well.

Coming full out, Simon sprang and practically flew through the air, grabbing the tree branch and swinging up, looking like a squirrel as he scrambled along it. When he jumped to the ground Jessie rushed to his side, furious with him.

"Where the hell have you been!" she cried.

The area around one eye was starting to swell, and a trickle of blood showed at the corner of his mouth. But he was grinning from ear to ear. "I was just having a little talk with the Terlin brothers." He chuckled with evil glee. "This time the conversation was much less one-sided."

"Then I'm sure they'll appreciate a chance to speak with you again," a voice said from behind them.

They all turned and looked. Nathan Lockheart stood there, a smug smile twisting his face. In his hand he held a pistol pointed in their direction.

"Come here, Jess, if indeed that is your

name." He sneered and waved her over with the gun. "I long to have you close to me again."

Jessie did as he said, and he put his arm around her waist, pulling her close and sticking the gun in her ribs. She gasped, and Simon took a step forward.

"Let her go, Lockheart."

The gun shifted back to point at Simon. "Stop right there." He peered through the shadows. "The infamous Simon Taylor." His beady eyes glanced from side to side, taking in the other two men. "And Paul. How nice to see you again. We have much to discuss. I assume Jess here and the other man are people you hired to help you take back your most enlightening documents?"

Paul was silent, staring at Lockheart hatefully.

"No answer? Never mind. I'm sure we'll get to the bottom of this." He indicated the fence with a motion of his head. "It was naughty of you to let my little boys out. They have tender constitutions, you know."

"Then I hope they eat something that disagrees with them," Paul said sarcastically.

Lockheart seemed to find that quite funny. "They probably will, Paul. They probably will."

Still keeping the gun trained on Simon, he released Jessie for a moment, took out a dog whistle, and blew on it. It made no sound, but there was a sudden flurry of noise from the underbrush to their left. He pulled Jessie close again, looking toward the sound with anticipation.

Simon's eyes met hers, and she shook her head slightly. From the small purse she carried she pulled out a little bottle, uncapped it, and tucked it carefully into the pocket of Nate's trousers—upside down.

Lockheart frowned as he felt something trickle down his leg. He pushed Jessie away. "What—"

The two dogs burst from the underbrush, wild-eyed and panting noisily. They took a brief, uninterested look at the rest of the group, then made a beeline for Lockheart.

"Little boys! Stop!"

They paid no attention. One of them jumped, a big brown blur, landing on his chest and knocking him down. The gun flew out of his hand, lost in the trees.

"Stop! Heel! What on earth are you doing!" Nate cried as the dogs pawed and snorted, climbing all over him. "Help! Oh, help! Somebody get them off me!"

The foursome paid no attention to his orders. Laughing hysterically, they quickly disappeared into the woods. From the highway somewhere up ahead of them, a forlorn wailing could be heard.

Breathing heavily, they jumped into their waiting car, Simon spinning its wheels on the

241

gravel shoulder as he pulled away from the Lockheart ranch.

"The cops?" Miles asked. "Why would he call the cops?"

"It's not the police." Simon slowed down as an ambulance went by going the other way. He grinned. "I thought the Terlin brothers might appreciate a little first aid," he explained, looking in his rearview mirror. "I told them to bring a lot of aspirin."

Paul was roaring with laughter in the backseat with Miles. "Nate will probably be able to use some too."

"I don't think," Miles added dryly, "that the dogs will take that as an excuse."

"What?"

"Not tonight, little boys," he said in a high-pitched voice. "I have a headache."

CHAPTER THIRTEEN

Though buoyed by their victory over Nathan Lockheart, the exhilarated foursome were very much aware they couldn't afford to celebrate yet. They had to get Paul and his papers to Harrold Stone as soon as possible. With that one goal in mind, they sped directly to the airport and grabbed the next flight back to New York.

Using assumed names, they checked into a hotel to get some much-needed rest. At first they were all too wound up to sleep, but the excitement finally gave way to exhaustion and they went to bed, with Paul and Miles in one room, Jessie and Simon in another. Once in bed, however, Jessie found she wasn't quite as exhausted as she thought she was.

Neither, obviously, was Simon. "Mmm. I thought you were sleepy," she murmured as his hands wandered sensuously over her.

"I thought I was too. But every time I close my eyes, they pop right open again. I keep re-

243

playing the events of today in my head." Simon pulled her tightly into his arms, the heat of his body making her feel as if she were melting, becoming one with him. "I suppose you're used to all this excitement."

Jessie turned her face to his, lightly kissing his cheek. "Some things you never get used to." She pressed her hips into his. "And some things you never get tired of."

"I was hoping you had some kind of remedy for insomnia," he replied with a wicked chuckle.

"There's always warm milk."

Simon nibbled on her neck, feeling her shuddering response. "I have something else in mind, as if you didn't know."

"It's a little difficult to miss," she said, wriggling seductively against his hard, masculine form. "And I wouldn't miss it for all the sleep in the world."

Their adrenaline was running high, increasing the sexual tension between them. They had made it, the danger was in the past, and yet that danger had made them even more aware of their growing feelings for each other. Urgently they sought the taste and touch of each other, burning with a thirst neither could quench. The exaltation of winning coursed through them, and the need to prove just how very much alive they were swept them into a maelstrom of passion, out of control, clinging to one another in loving abandon.

Sensation washed over them, wave after wave, until the lovers thought a moment more would surely cause them to lose their minds. Heated flesh against heated flesh, they embraced in wild and urgent passion, taking of each other greedily. Arching her body to his, Jessie gave as well, offering herself to him, eager to capture that final flash of fire within herself.

Another wave of desire swept through her afterward, as Simon tenderly stroked her, touching her face in reverent joy. Sleep was the furthest thing from their minds now. Only passion remained, a deep and consuming need that overwhelmed them again and again during the long night ahead. When at last they did fall asleep, truly exhausted now, they slept knowing that the excitement they had shared this night could never compare to the excitement they found every time they touched. It was a feeling far more powerful than fear or danger, and deep enough to last a lifetime.

Jessie awoke in Simon's arms and allowed herself a few happy moments of gazing at his sleeping face before gently untangling herself. She was tempted to wake him, communicate her desire and love in the most delicious way possible. But he looked so peaceful, and she had things she had to do first anyway.

Quietly slipping on her robe, she then went into the adjoining sitting room and called Harrold Stone, making her report quick and concise. All he needed now were the basics, and she wanted to get back into bed with Simon before he woke up.

After hearing her out and commending her for work well done, however, Stone did some talking of his own. As Jessie listened, a deep frown furrowed her brow and all thoughts of an amorous start to this day disappeared. Her job wasn't finished. She had yet one more role to play, and this one would test her abilities to the limit.

"Jessie?" Stone asked, worried by her prolonged silence.

"I'm still here," she replied bleakly.

"Can you do it? Or perhaps I should ask, will you do it?" he amended.

"I wish you hadn't asked me to in the first place, Harrold, but you know me. Once I start something, I finish it." Would Simon understand that? "Yes, I'll do it."

Simon walked in just as Jessie hung up the phone. She slipped a piece of paper with an address and phone number on it into the pocket of her robe and smiled at him.

"Good morning, sleepyhead."

Simon gazed at her, noticed the slight tension around the corners of her mouth. "Something wrong?" he asked.

"Now, what could be wrong?" She stood up and went to him, hugging him fiercely. "Sleep well?"

Simon yawned, then fixed her with a look of sensual invitation. "I slept fine. It was the way I woke up I didn't like."

"Oh?" Had he overheard her phone conversation?

"I had expected to have you in my arms when I opened my eyes." He pulled her even tighter into his embrace, grinning roguishly. "Why don't we go back to bed and start the day right?"

The very idea made her pulse race. She kissed him soundly, almost gave in to temptation, then pulled away. "I can't. I have to get Paul and his papers to—to a safe place first."

Simon released her reluctantly, nodding his head in agreement. "Yes, I suppose you're right." He winked at her. "Business before pleasure."

"Why don't you go ahead and take a shower? I'll call room service and get us some breakfast."

"I have a better idea," he replied, taking her hand and pulling her toward the bathroom. "Why don't we take a shower together?"

Jessie retrieved her hand and prodded him along with her finger. "You're incorrigible!" she exclaimed, forcing a lightness to her voice she certainly didn't feel. "I'll wake Miles and Paul, then we can go and get this over with."

Simon shrugged and disappeared into the bathroom. When the water started running, Jessie picked up the phone again. First she ordered breakfast, then she called Miles, and then she got to the real reason she had wanted Simon out of the room.

She took the slip of paper from her pocket and dialed the number Harrold Stone had given her. A man answered.

"I have something you want," she said.

"Who is this?" the man asked.

"That doesn't matter. I have Paul Taylor and a certain set of very enlightening documents. I am prepared to turn both over to you—for a price. Interested?"

There was a pause, and for a moment Jessie thought he was going to hang up. Then he said, "I am indeed very interested. Where shall we meet?"

Jessie gave him the address Stone had given her and then named a nice round number. "Those are the only arrangements to be made," she said gruffly. "I'll bring the goods, you bring the cash. If you're not there by eleven-thirty I'll take my offer elsewhere."

She hung up, overcome with a feeling of dread. The stage was set and the players soon would take their positions, but she had the uneasy feeling Simon wouldn't like this little production one bit.

With the premium placed on commercial storage space in crowded urban areas, abandoned warehouses were largely myths. A few quiet, disused buildings did exist, though, and were excellent places to transact the kind of business Jessie had in mind. Paul got edgier by the moment as the tone of the neighborhood became apparent. Frowning, he lapsed into nervous silence. Miles obviously had a great many questions too from the way he kept looking at her, but he kept them to himself and drove on. Simon, on the other hand, voiced his concerns quite strongly.

"Where the hell are we going?" he demanded.

"To a meeting," Jessie replied.

"Down here?" Simon looked out the window in disgust. "Your employer has a macabre sense of humor."

"He thinks there may be someone in his own office who might snatch Paul away from us," she explained. Her voice had the ring of truth, as well it should. Harrold Stone did indeed suspect someone, had even supplied her with his phone number. "He decided it would be best to keep Paul under wraps for a while."

They pulled up in front of a dilapidated building and got out, stepping over refuse to get through the narrow front door. Inside, amid rows of crates, the musty aura of the place assaulted them. It was quiet except for the disconcerting sound of something scurrying in some dark corner. Sunlight filtered through gray windows thick with grime. Their footsteps sounded hollow and made dust rise and vibrate in the air.

"Lovely," Miles commented.

"Yeah," Paul agreed. "If I didn't trust you guys . . ."

A voice came from somewhere off to the side, startling everyone except Jessie. It was the man she had talked to on the phone.

"Who are all these people?" he asked.

Jessie peered into the dusty gloom, making out a shape behind some nearby crates. She pointed to her tense companions one by one. "This is Miles, he's with me. Paul Taylor, and his brother, Simon." Her eyes met Simon's, trying to communicate something to him. He was staring at her with so much confusion and suspicion she doubted he noticed her silent warning.

"I only wanted Paul and his documents," the man said tersely.

"I couldn't get Paul away from his brother without arousing suspicion," Jessie replied. "Simon has the papers, and he's dangerous."

"I knew it," Paul said, disgust contorting his

features. "I knew she was too good to be true." He glared at Jessie with ugly contempt.

Simon turned to her. "Jessie—"

"Shut up!" the man said. "If he moves," he told someone off to the side, "shoot him."

Jessie tried to ignore the pain she saw in Simon's eyes. Her plan was working perfectly. She knew she could trust Miles to follow her lead, but Paul's outrage and Simon's confusion had to be real. As long as she kept tight control of the situation, no one would get hurt.

She swallowed thickly, keeping her voice even. "You do and Miles will shoot you," she said. "The deal is for Paul and his papers. Simon won't interrupt again."

Simon couldn't interrupt. His anger at this betrayal made him speechless. All he could do was look at Jessie, his eyes twin pools of fury. She had been lying all along! Everything she had said and done had been an act, a ruse to get Paul and his papers together in one place so she could make some obscene deal.

"Whatever you say," the man said as he stepped from his hiding place.

If there really was anyone with him, Jessie couldn't tell, but she knew better than to assume he was alone. She looked at him, a ferret-faced individual in a blue pinstripe suit. It wasn't anyone she knew or had seen in Harrold

Stone's office, but then she had only met a handful of his staff.

A quick glance at Paul told her he didn't know the man either. Simon was still glaring at her, and Miles's eyes never left the man standing in front of them.

"That's right," she said, toughening her voice. "Whatever I say. Now let's quit playing hide and seek and get this over with."

The man pulled a suitcase from behind another crate and patted it, then held up his hand. "I'm anxious to complete our arrangement too, but I admit to being confused. You are Harrold Stone's hired hand, are you not?"

Jessie laughed harshly. "Harrold is a fine man, but he doesn't pay very well."

He seemed to think that over. "Yes, in these uncertain times I myself have found it beneficial to have a secondary source of income."

"I had heard as much," Jessie said.

"From whom?"

She shrugged carelessly. "Word gets around."

"Yes," the man admitted slyly. "I suppose it does. Still, with Paul here in my keeping I'll be able to set my own price. My job with the SEC will have to be terminated, but as you said, Harrold doesn't pay very well."

"But Paul's company does?" she asked.

"Exactly. Which brings to mind another question. Why didn't you go directly to them?"

For the first time, Miles spoke up. His tone was just as casual and convincing as Jessie's. "Because they tried to have us killed, that's why," he said.

"Yes, I heard about that," the man remarked. "Most fortunate you got away. Otherwise we wouldn't all be here doing business now."

Paul snorted in disgust. "They sold us out, Simon. And I thought they were our friends."

"So did I, big brother," Simon replied, pain evident in his voice. "So did I."

Jessie looked at him, then had to turn away. "Let's get on with this," she said, trying to keep her voice from cracking with emotion.

"Yes, let's. Paul, please retrieve your documents from your brother and bring them here." The man waved a hand to remind them of his unseen protection. "And do be careful, gentlemen."

They did as they were told. Jessie stepped over to check the suitcase as the man looked over the papers. She smiled and nodded. "I'm satisfied," she said.

"So am I." He looked at Paul. "Your company will be happy too, Paul. I'm saving them money, really. The principals in this little deal were all preparing for an extended stay in another country, an expensive proposition when one considers the cost of keeping one step ahead of extradition."

Jessie stepped away, tilted her head back, and yelled, "How about you, Harrold? Are you satisfied?"

The sound of her voice had barely stopped echoing through the building when a flurry of activity surrounded them. Heavy footsteps came from all sides, men popped out of crates holding firearms of all sorts, and one hard, steady voice rang out.

"Police! Everyone stay exactly where you are!"

It was the voice of authority, and even Jessie stood very still. The chaos soon settled down and a stern-looking policeman walked a rather innocuous-looking man out from behind a crate. He was handcuffed, a predicament that soon befell the rogue SEC employee as well. They were led out of the building at gunpoint.

Two men strolled over to Jessie from a dark corner. One of them was Harrold Stone. "Hello, Jessie," he said calmly. He nodded at Miles. "Thank you both. I had suspected that man of taking bribes for some time but didn't have the proof. Now he'll get what he deserves."

Jessie smiled. "You're a tricky man, Harrold. From the beginning you were more interested in catching that guy than you were in the stock scam."

Harrold Stone made an apologetic gesture with his big hands. "Just keeping my own department clean, Jessie." He glanced at Simon and Paul. "I think you have some explaining to do."

Jessie turned to Simon, anxious to straighten things out. But Simon didn't look confused. In fact, his face held little emotion at all. He was staring at Jessie as if she were an alien and he was waiting to see what it would do next.

"You used us," he said flatly. "You wanted us to look properly surprised and angry, so you could continue to play your little games."

"To be fair, Mr. Taylor," Harrold said, "she was acting under my orders. We decided it would be safer for all concerned if you and your brother knew nothing of this setup."

"Is my brother under arrest?"

Harrold pursed his lips. "Not officially. But we are going to take him in for a statement. He has a lot to answer for."

"Then let's go and get that done."

Harrold nodded and the man beside him stepped over and took Paul gently by the arm, leading him out of the building. "You can go with him if you like."

Simon turned back to Jessie. "Yes, I'll go with him. There isn't anything here I want any-more."

"Simon—"

"No," he interrupted quietly. "No more. I don't want any of your explanations or excuses."

He turned on his heel and followed Harrold Stone outside.

A policeman spoke quietly into a walkie-talkie for a moment, then he and the last of his men left as well. Miles and Jessie stood looking at one another. Though his expression was compassionate for the desperation he saw on her face, his eyes were hard.

"Jessie," he said quietly, "there have been times in our long association when I have been angry, frustrated, even downright furious with you. But this is the first time since that night I caught you with those jewels that I've felt like turning you over my knee."

"I was just doing my job," she objected.

"Then I hope you like it as much as you think you do," he said, turning to leave. "Because your job may very well be the only thing you have left."

CHAPTER FOURTEEN

"That's right," Simon told the young man he was helping. "Keep the muscles in your foot tight when you kick. If you don't the shock is transmitted to your knee joint." He watched him try the movement again, nodding. "Good. Remember, form before speed."

The pair bowed to each other, then Simon went to the next pupil in line, correcting his stance. The line increased in rank from neophytes to advanced students. As Simon went along he became more critical, his instructions less gentle, a light touch to check a white belt's balance turning into a lightning-quick attempt to shove a brown belt to the mat.

As he was leading them through a repetitious series of movements, a visitor to the *dojo* caught his eye. He turned to the highest-ranking student and bowed.

"Continue," he said curtly. She returned his bow and took over the class.

Simon walked over to the visitor, his face calm. Inside, however, he was in turmoil, a mixture of longing and suspicion tearing at him.

"Jessie," he said in way of greeting.

"Hello, Simon. I didn't mean to interrupt."

Simon looked at her, his heart aching. He had seen her face in his dreams every night for the past week, but his dreams couldn't compare with having her right there in front of him.

"Class is nearly over," he said.

She smiled and looked at the row of hard-working students. "I should hope so. They look about ready to drop."

"Why are you here?" He wanted her there, wanted to touch her, but at the same time a hard shield had been lowered over his heart.

She had helped Paul, had been instrumental in seeing that Harrold Stone had treated his brother fairly. Paul would never sell stocks and bonds again, but at least he hadn't pulled any jail time, which was more than could be said of Nathan Lockheart and the others. As a matter of fact, Jessie had even tugged some strings and gotten Paul a job as a financial consultant.

He couldn't forget how she had used them both, continued playing her dangerous games right to the very end. He wanted to take her in his arms, hold her and tell her everything was all right. But he wasn't sure everything *was* all right. How much of what they had shared had been a game to her as well?

"Simon, we need to talk," Jessie said, suppressing the urge to reach out and touch him. He looked hard, almost rigid.

"About what?"

His voice was so cold, so full of suspicion. "I know you don't have any reason to believe anything I say. But please, can't we go somewhere and talk?" she asked. "I've missed you."

And I've missed you, sweet Jessie, he thought. But he said gruffly, "What's the matter, Jessie? Business been slow?"

She sighed heavily and closed her eyes, leaning against the wall behind her. "I don't know how much more of this I can take. Miles is angry with me, you're angry with me. *I'm* angry with me too. We all have a perfect right to hate Jessie McMillan right now."

"I don't hate you, Jessie," Simon said softly. "I just don't trust you."

"Damn," she muttered, opening her eyes. "I haven't been sleeping, the flight down here was lousy, and if I don't talk to *someone* I'm going to go right out of my mind!" She looked into his eyes, her voice rough with emotion. "Tar and feather me, drown me in your pool, do whatever you like but please, please talk to me!"

Simon felt the barrier around his heart slip a little. Maybe this, too, was an act, but he didn't think so. "All right. Let me change and I'll be right with you."

She followed him to his house, the sight of the place touching a sore spot in her heart. A sharp sense of loss struck her when she stepped inside. There was the pool where she had first felt the sensuous touch of Simon's hands, the kitchen where they had shared such camaraderie while making their plans for retrieving Paul's papers. Down the hall was the bedroom where they had made love and shared something much deeper. It was real, the memory painfully clear in her mind.

She loved him. She felt certain her love was returned, or had been until she had pulled that last trick on him. How could one grievous error in judgment take all that away from her? She had to make him listen if she could, but she could tell it wasn't going to be easy.

At his school he had been calm and controlled. Now Simon seemed tense. Was he perhaps thinking of the same things she was? She hoped so. She wanted him to think about the good times they shared, the laughter, the sensuality. He had asked her a question once, and that question came back to haunt her now. *Will I ever know the real Jessie McMillan?*

She sat on the couch, Simon in a chair opposite her. He was looking at her expectantly, his tension directed outward in anger.

"Well? You came all this way to talk, so talk."

"I wanted to apologize for the way I used you and Paul," she began. "I should have told you my plans."

"Yes, you should have. Apology accepted." He looked into her eyes for a moment, then turned away. Having her there was about to drive him crazy. She was so close and beautiful, how much longer could he stand not to touch her?

"Anything else?" he asked impatiently.

"Just one thing," she replied, then paused, waiting until he returned his eyes to hers. "I wanted you to know that I love you."

Startled, he frowned, then stood up and went to look out the window at the pool. "Who are you, Jessie?" he asked. "What role are you playing today? Do you even know yourself?"

"Simon—"

He turned and angrily interrupted her. "I know you were only doing your job, but you're too damn good at taking risks, assuming roles, and pretending you're somebody else. And lying to your friends," he added, pointing a finger in accusation. "Is this just another act you're trying to add to your repertoire?"

"Damn you!" she cried, springing to her feet and going to confront him. "Don't you think I've been tortured enough for one lousy mistake? I'm not making any excuses, Simon. I went a step too far in doing my job and I know it." Did

261

she ever. Every time Miles looked at her she saw the accusation in his eyes. Simon was looking at her the same way.

"Don't tell me you've seen the error of your ways?" Simon asked sarcastically.

"Seen them? I've had them very nearly etched upon my brain in the past week." She threw her hands in the air in a gesture of hopelessness. "What's the use? You don't believe a word I'm saying anyway." Turning away from him, Jessie felt hot tears sting her eyes.

Simon couldn't take any more. He reached out and put his hands on her shoulders, turning her back to face him. "Jessie, look at me. I believe you when you say you're sorry for using Paul and me. Heaven knows you made up for it as far as Paul is concerned. He thinks you hung the moon."

Impatiently brushing at the tears streaming down her cheeks, Jessie met his eyes, saw the warmth there. "Then why . . ."

"Why did I walk away from you in New York?" He shrugged helplessly. "Pride. Doubt." Simon held her at arms' length, searching her eyes, almost afraid of what he might find there. "Did I ever really know you, Jessie? Was any part of what we shared real?"

She pushed his arms aside and hugged him, reveling in the feel of his body pressed against hers. "It was all real, Simon," she replied, her voice roughened by tears. "I'm real, here and now. This is real."

Jessie tilted her head and kissed him, her lips pliant yet demanding, trying to communicate all the love she felt in a single touch. In that touch Simon felt the truth, a truth words alone could never convey. With a force that overwhelmed them both he wrapped his arms around her, holding her tightly lest she disappear. When their lips parted, he gazed once more into those lovely eyes.

"I love you, Jessie," he murmured huskily. "Art dealer, thief, or even the crazy woman preoccupied with danger, I love them all. I love them because I love you, and deep down you're all those things."

She shook her head. "No. You are the only one who has ever seen the real me, Simon." She smiled, feeling as though she would explode with joy. "Hopelessly in love, mixed up and frightened and scared to death of losing you. I love you, Simon. I love you so very much."

"I've missed you, sweet Jessie." He swung her into his arms, wanting to possess her and knowing now that it was possible. She was his at long last. He would never let her go.

"Prove it," Jessie whispered in his ear. "Prove how much you've missed me, Simon, my love. And I'll prove just how very real I am."

With slow steps they walked toward the bedroom, holding hands, whispering soft encouragements. There was no hurry now. Their time apart made them want to savor each touch, cherish each word. Simon had come so close to losing her, all due to his stubborn pride, and he vowed not to let it stand in his way again. Jessie was the only woman he would ever need, to have her close beside him day after day for years to come. Looking into her shining eyes, he could feel his love being returned to him.

Unbuttoning his shirt, Jessie leaned closer to him, inhaling his male scent, dipping her head to taste the salty skin of his chest, her lips teasing each nipple in turn. Marveling at the response of his body to her touch, his quickening heartbeat was music to her ears. She made a vow of her own. No more dangerous games. Simon was here for her, and she wanted to be near him always. He made her feel more of a woman than she had ever felt in her life, softer, more feminine, yet stronger and self-assured.

Undressing each other slowly, they tasted and touched, breathing each other's scent. With a gentleness neither had ever experienced, they made love, the tenderness of each passing moment making them feel suspended in time. Stunned by their love, weakened by the powerful emotions they shared, the impassioned lovers clung to each other, their movements slowly carrying them to the brink of ecstasy and beyond. Side by side, their hearts beating as one, a profound sense of peace at last settled over them.

"Yes," Simon whispered in her ear. "You're real, Jessie. I don't know how I could have ever doubted you."

Jessie covered his face with tiny, sweet kisses. "You had good reason, I realize that now. But I promise to never give you reason to doubt me again."

Simon admired Jessie as she strolled gracefully across the yard toward the house. Just thinking about her brought his senses alive. He could still feel those long legs, silky smooth, caressing and wrapping around him, making him as much a part of herself as she was a part of him.

He watched through the kitchen window as she plucked flowers from the garden, graceful, smooth, raising each one to inhale the scent and feel the texture against her face. That face, the only one he ever wanted or needed to wake up to for the rest of their lives.

He thought of her lips on his; the feeling was so strong he could almost taste them. The heat in him was rising by the moment, burning as hot as the sun that danced upon her shoulders. She dug her toes into the grass one last time before stepping onto the concrete skirting of the pool, then arranged her flowers in a vase on the table.

She turned her back to him, slowly stretched, well aware of her silent observer. Feeling his eyes upon her, Jessie untied her bikini top, letting it fall to the ground as she walked toward the cool, inviting water of the pool.

Simon was on his feet and out the patio door in a flash. "Jessie! What are you doing?"

She boldly turned to face him. "You don't know?"

"Someone might see you," he chastised, his heart racing at the sight of her.

"You didn't seem concerned about that last night." She took a step backward, teasing him, staying just out of his reach as he advanced upon her.

"That's because it was dark last night," he replied, moving toward her, his gaze running up and down her shapely form. "The sight of those lovely breasts are for me alone."

"My, such possessiveness."

"You had better get used to it," he grumbled, stalking her as she edged around the pool away from him. His eyes widened as she hooked her thumbs into the waistband of her bikini bottoms. "Jessie . . ." His voice trailed off in warning.

Jessie inched the remaining half of her suit down a little. She grinned. "Nobody can see. Believe me, I know the best vantage points for spying on this house," she said with a wave of her hand, "and no one is looking. Unless one of your neighbors has drilled a hole in the fence."

"What if somebody has a telescope or—"

"Such a vivid imagination! Do you have a telescope?" she teased. She slipped the suit down a bit lower.

Simon stopped a few feet from her, taking in the lovely sight before him. Firm, proud breasts taunting him, a slender waist flaring into shapely hips, covered now only by a scrap of turquoise material. Long, beautiful legs . . .

"Simon?" He didn't look up, obviously lost deep in his own wicked thoughts. "Earth to Simon," she taunted softly. "This is Jessie. I am about to take off."

He watched, hypnotized as she slipped off the tiny bit of turquoise cloth, an inch at a time, slowly and sensuously downward.

"Catch!" she cried playfully, tossing the bottom of her bikini in his direction. Startled, he grabbed for it or, rather, fell for it—right into the pool.

He came up spluttering and splashing. "Blast you, Jessie McMillan! When I get hold of you . . ."

Jessie danced around the pool, childlike, pointing and shrieking with laughter. "Gotcha!" But she was very much a woman as she leaned over and taunted him with her uncovered form.

He smiled, treading water in the middle of

the pool. "Very funny. Now help me out," he said, his voice syrupy sweet.

Jessie shook her head. "I see the vengeance in those eyes, Simon. I'm not about to fall for that old trick." She sat down on the grass, wrapping her arms around her knees, chuckling gleefully.

"Jessie . . ."

"Yes, love?"

"Just because you've got the advantage now . . ."

"Aren't you a little overdressed for swimming?"

"I'm starting a new trend." He slipped below the surface, his eyes gleaming. "Help! I'm sinking!"

She shook her head. "I'm not falling for that, either. If you're sinking, take your pants off. After all, you do have such gorgeous legs."

"You'd let me drown?" he asked in a wounded tone.

"Never."

He stopped pretending and started trying to unzip his pants. "As soon . . . as I get out . . . I'm going to make you pay for this!" He slipped and plunged underwater again, came up gasping for air. "This is impossible!"

"Need some help?" she inquired sweetly, looking very fetching as she crawled over to the side of the pool. She wasn't worried. He wouldn't drown, and neither would he be able to get his pants off. Wet zippers *were* impossible.

Simon watched her advance toward him, resting his chin on his forearms as he hung on the pool's edge. "Come on in, the water's fine."

"And have you dunk me? No, thanks," she returned, eyeing him suspiciously.

"No faith. Don't you trust me?"

"Hah!"

He looked crestfallen. "And here I thought you were trying to seduce me."

"I was."

"Was? You don't want me anymore?"

"Of course I want you."

"Then you'd better save me," Simon said ominously, his head disappearing from view. "Because I really am . . ."

Jessie peered over the edge of the pool, watching bubbles rise to the surface. "Simon? I'm not falling for this." She inched closer, starting to frown. "Simon?"

She screamed when he came flashing to the surface like a porpoise, grabbing her arms and flipping her over his head to the center of the pool. She came up spewing water.

"What a dirty trick!"

"Just good clean fun," he objected. He swam over to her. "Need some swimming lessons? Or maybe some lessons on how to tell when an opponent is about to strike?"

"I'll strike you, you . . . Oh!" She gasped when he pressed himself against her. "How did you get your pants off?"

"Does it matter?" he whispered in her ear.

Jessie moaned softly, luxuriating in the slippery, sensuous feel of his body against hers. "No."

"I love you, Jessie."

"I love you, Simon. With all my heart and soul."

Keeping them both afloat with his powerful legs, his hands glided over her delicious curves. "And body?"

"Mmm. Especially my body. I'm all yours," she murmured against his lips as they kissed.

"Life with you will be anything but dull, Jessie McMillan." He paused, looking into her eyes. "Which reminds me . . ."

Jessie read his thoughts. "Jessie McMillan Taylor," she said. "Has a nice ring to it."

"Jessie *Aberdeen* McMillan Taylor," Simon corrected.

Her mouth dropped open. "How did you know my middle name? Even Miles doesn't know it!"

"I have my sources," Simon replied smugly.

Jessie shook her head in wonder. "It will take me a lifetime to figure you out, Simon."

"We have that lifetime before us, Jessie. I mean to use it to the fullest."

She rubbed against him. "Starting now?"

"Here and now, my love. Here and now." Simon got out of the pool, wrapping a towel around himself and holding one for Jessie. She teased him unmercifully with her slick, wet body as she climbed from the water, then draped the towel around her.

"The sun feels so good." She sighed, leaning against him. "Let's enjoy it for a while."

"Only if you put on a suit, you shameless wench." He retrieved it for her, watched hungrily as she put it on.

"And now you have to put yours on," she demanded playfully. "You're not the only one with a possessive streak."

Side by side in the sun, they watched as the water evaporated from their skin then turned the sensible act of applying suntan oil into a sensuous game. Totally relaxed, their minds played upon the step they were about to take.

"Do you think Miles would be my best man?" Simon asked.

"He'll be too busy giving the bride away."

He grinned. "You're right. That would be a job he would insist upon doing."

"Simon?" Jessie propped herself up on one elbow to look at him. Though her voice was lazy, her eyes were suddenly serious.

"Yes, love?"

"I know you haven't asked this question yet,

but I think it's time we thought about it." She paused, trying to think of how to broach the subject. "My work—"

He interrupted her by reaching out and putting a finger to her lips. "It's not that I haven't thought about it, Jessie. I haven't asked because I'm not going to ask. I told you I loved you, all of you, and that includes what you do for a living."

"Thank you." She smiled, not really surprised that he was leaving the decision up to her. That was the kind of man he was, and she loved him for it. "I know you're not thrilled by the idea of me flirting with danger."

He smiled wryly and kissed the tip of her nose. "I'm sure it doesn't thrill you to think about me getting into the ring with a guy who can break bricks with his head either, now does it?"

"No," she admitted. "But as long as I'm with you, where I can leap into the fray and protect you, I can live with it."

Simon laughed at the image. "I feel the same way. If you insist on taking dangerous assignments, then I'll insist on going with you."

"Then I won't take any dangerous assignments," Jessie replied quietly.

"Jessie . . ."

"I'm serious. I've thought about it, and come to the decision I don't want that kind of excitement anymore." She stroked his firm thigh. "You're all the excitement I need."

Looking at her warily, Simon remarked, "Me and the occasional task of locating somebody or something, you mean?"

She laughed. "You're getting to know me pretty well, aren't you?"

"Not as well as I'm going to." He leaned closer and chewed lightly on her earlobe. "It's a deal, then. You'll always be at ringside, and I'll be your apprentice locator."

"But I told you! No more dangerous assignments."

"And I told *you*," he replied amiably, "I'll be there to make sure you don't fall back into old habits. No more flirting with danger, and no more flirting with strange men, either. The Nathan Lockhearts of the world will have to be brought to justice by some other means."

"Hah!" she cried. "So that's the real reason you want to join the team."

"Darn right. The only man I want you chasing after for the next hundred years or so is me."

Jessie grinned, feeling a warm glow that had nothing to do with the bright sunlight beating down upon her. "Okay, it's a deal. I have to admit I have an ulterior motive for being with you too," she said. "I have to make sure no strange women pick you up outside the dressing room."

"No way," he promised, unable to resist the opportunity to tease her. "Look at the trouble that got me into the last time."

In his mind's eye Simon once again saw Jessie standing by the dressing room doors, a lovely mysterious vision who had worked her way into his life—and worked her magic on his heart. Soon, she would become his wife, and he couldn't be happier.

"Do you remember that autograph you gave me?" she asked.

"I do," he replied. " 'To Jessie, the most beautiful liar I ever met.' We should probably have it framed."

"No. Frame this instead." She kissed him, a lingering kiss full of total commitment. "Just you, me and our love for each other. There will be no more lies between us ever again."

My darling," he whispered. Jessie felt
warmth cover Matt and was going down over
brittle ice.

Then dragged her. And near her. Tears ran
down the ocean place, Jessie was right were
new of that it hot, away and moving and the
window. She turned around and got her hands
and careful even putting himself and, men were
the horizontal. Throws we and of the gesture.

CHAPTER FIFTEEN

Jessie gazed out the window at the pristine carpet of snow surrounding the cabin. She sighed, more at peace than she could remember being in her entire life. No telephone interrupted the silence. Harrold Stone and others like him would have to do without her talents for a while longer.

She hadn't had time to miss her work. Simon saw to that. It was more exciting just sitting beside the fire with him than any hair-raising assignment she had ever undertaken.

"Cabin fever?" Simon asked softly as he came up behind her. He wrapped his arms around her and kissed the back of her neck.

She laughed and leaned into his embrace, resting her head on his shoulder and kissing his cheek. "No. I miss the pool, though."

"You're not missing much. I just heard on the radio that Dallas got its first ice storm of the season. The whole city is paralyzed."

"No stamina," she observed haughtily. "You wouldn't catch Manhattan closing down over a little ice."

Simon hugged her. "And they say Texans are big braggarts."

"On the other hand, New York snow was never that white," she said, pointing out the window. She turned around and put her hands on his shoulders, pulling herself up to plant a kiss on his forehead. "I guess we found the perfect place."

"Anywhere you are is the perfect place for me."

Jessie melted against him. "I couldn't agree more."

They went to sit beside the fire, Jessie swinging her legs up to rest them on his lap. She leaned back on the soft cushions and sighed.

"Happy?" Simon asked.

"I think ecstatic would come closer to how I feel."

"Me too. It's a shame we're almost out of groceries. We'll have to go back to civilization soon."

Jessie poked his hard, flat stomach with one finger and chuckled throatily. "I thought you could live on love?"

"Not when you drive me to such extraordinary heights of passion," he replied dramatically, grabbing her hand and nibbling on her wrist. "I need all my strength to keep you happy."

"Oh, yes. My love slave. You don't need to be driven very far to get carried away with passion." His tongue traced a pattern across the sensitive skin of her palm and she felt a warmth creeping over her. "We could forage for nuts and berries."

Simon made a face. "Not unless we can find a T-bone steak bush."

"If there is one, you'll have to wrestle the bears to get to it."

"They're hibernating." He made a grab for her and they rolled off the couch, landing on the soft carpet in a tangled, hysterical heap. "Besides, I'd rather wrestle you."

Jessie tempted him with the movement of her hips. "I think you've got me pinned already."

They had tried to find the limits of their desire and love for one another, but kept discovering new heights. All they wanted was to be with each other, touching and being touched, quiet moments alone with scarcely a need to speak. They shared such a moment now, lying side by side, watching the flames leap in the fireplace, knowing their love burned just as brightly.

"What's that noise?" Jessie asked curiously. She raised her head and listened as the noise grew louder, closer. She had become so accustomed to the silence there that the noise seemed an abominable intrusion.

Simon frowned. "Sounds like a helicopter."

"Just passing over?"

"I don't think so," he replied ominously. "Look." He sat up and pointed to the window, where Jessie could see snow being whipped against the cabin. "I think it's coming in to land."

They got up and went to look outside, getting to the window just in time to see the aircraft settle gently to earth in the clearing a hundred yards away. The noise quieted down and the rotor slowed. A man dressed in a bulky coat got out, ducking his head as he ran under the blades. He was soon knocking on the door of the cabin.

Curious but cautious, the pair went to investigate, Simon motioning for her to stay behind him. He opened the door, and his eyes widened in surprise.

"Hello. I wonder if you would be interested in a subscription to *National Geographic?*"

"Miles!" Jessie cried.

"Come in before you freeze, you idiot," Simon said, grinning broadly as he ushered him inside and closed the door. "I didn't know you were a pilot too."

Miles was pulling off his coat by the fire. Jessie was assisting him. "Miles is a man of many talents." She went to get him a cup of hot coffee.

"Don't I know it," Simon remarked in a good-natured mutter. "He probably stole the chopper."

"I'll pretend I didn't hear that," Miles said. He looked around the cozy cabin, nodding appreciatively. "Nice little love nest you have here. What do you do for entertainment when you're not enjoying wedded bliss?" he asked with a sly chuckle. "Sit and listen to the rocks erode?"

"No, wait for unexpected visitors to drop from the sky," Simon replied. "I'm almost afraid to ask, but just what are you doing so far from a state with legalized gambling?"

Miles sighed. "There you go again, questioning my motives. I'm shocked, I really am."

Jessie returned from the kitchen with coffee for them all. "Is Simon impugning your character again?" she asked.

"He certainly is. I would have thought you'd have him trained by now."

"Hey!" Simon objected.

"Some men are harder to train than others," Jessie replied, patting Simon on the knee. "For instance, I still haven't got you trained to come to the point."

"I beg your pardon?"

"Come on, Miles. Spill it."

He laughed. "You mean you don't believe I'm just here for a visit?"

"In a word, no. You complain when the thermometer dips below seventy. Whatever brought you into snow country, it wasn't the urge to sit and chat."

Miles winked at Simon. "Infuriating little beast, isn't she?"

"She can be." Simon grabbed her hand before she could poke him for his remark. "Luckily, I'm faster than she is."

"Wait till you've known her for ten years."

"Miles . . ."

He shrugged. "Okay, here's the story. A major motion picture studio is requesting your services, Jessie. It seems this prima donna starlet, in a fit of pique, has taken off with every single copy of the script for her latest blockbuster. The picture is over budget and under a heavy completion deadline." He arched his eyebrows and looked at her pointedly. "They want you to get the scripts and the reluctant actress back, in good shape and preferably in good humor."

"Hmmm," Jessie hummed thoughtfully. "Tall order."

Simon looked at her and frowned. "Jessie . . ."

"Should be pretty simple, actually," Miles interjected. "I'm given to understand that all the young lady needs is a sympathetic ear and a bit of cajoling. Once you find her, that is," he added.

Jessie glanced at Simon, grinning impishly. "Sort of sounds like fun."

"Sure," Simon remarked sardonically. "The last time you said that, I nearly got beaten to a pulp and you had a gun poked in your ribs."

"Now, Simon," Jessie coaxed, moving closer and putting her arm around his shoulder, "you know you really enjoyed yourself. You told me you found the whole break-in at Lockheart's ranch very exhilarating."

He grinned sheepishly, then caught himself and scowled. "Almost getting hit by a bus gets your heart going faster too, but that doesn't mean you want it to happen again."

"Ah, yes." Miles sighed, leaning back in his chair. "The thrill of the chase, the sweet taste of victory, the—"

"The two of you trussed up in the back of a car," Simon interrupted, trying not to laugh.

"This isn't the same kind of job," Jessie said. "I told you I wasn't going to do any of the dangerous stuff any more and I meant it."

Miles stood up, took a photograph from his coat pocket, and handed it to Simon. "And just look at the fringe benefits."

"Wow!" Simon studied the picture of the curvaceous starlet. "Well, maybe it wouldn't hurt to just see if we can find her." He showed Jessie the picture, and she kicked him on the shin. "Ouch!"

"I've changed my mind," she said, crossing her arms defiantly. "I won't do it."

"Please?" Miles got down on his knees, his hands clasped in front of him. "Pretty please with sugar on it? You found your true love this way, the least you can do is give me the same opportunity," he pleaded. "I'll do all the leg work."

Simon chuckled and took another look at the cheesecake photo. "Looks as if there's quite a bit of leg work to do, all right." This time he blocked her foot before Jessie could kick him.

"Of course," Miles continued, "if you don't think you can trust your husband . . ."

"I can trust him, all right," she said, giving Simon a warning glance. "I just won't let him come along."

"Oh, no, you don't." Simon gave her an equally threatening look. "Remember our deal. You can still pursue your crazy vocation, as long as you don't take on dangerous assignments—and provided I come along as your bodyguard."

"Who is going to guard you from *her* body?" Jessie asked, taking the photograph away from him.

Miles snatched the picture back and held it to his chest. "He wouldn't dare touch the woman I love."

"Oh, Miles! You don't even know her."

"That didn't stop you from falling in love with Simon," he reminded her indignantly. "I've seen all of her movies. I worship her from afar, you might say."

They all laughed, then Simon looked at her, his expression serious. "It's up to you, Jessie."

She knew he really meant it and felt her love for him grow even stronger. He wouldn't let her risk her life, and she would never allow herself to get into that position again. They cherished each other too much to take foolish risks.

He knew her and knew how much she craved what Miles had termed the thrill of the chase. Simon loved her too much to treat her like a bird in a gilded cage. He loved all of her, including her ferocious independence.

Jessie smiled at him, then leaned forward and kissed him soundly. "Let's go find us a movie star."

"Hooray!" Miles jumped up and started putting on his coat. "I'll help you pack. That bird out there costs a bundle every hour whether it's in the air or not."

He left the room, muttering excitedly. Jessie and Simon stood up, wrapping their arms around each other.

"I guess the honeymoon's over, huh?" Jessie asked.

"Never. Life with you is one perpetual honeymoon."

She rewarded him with a kiss that promised unending love and delight. "You're sure you don't mind going on this little jaunt?" she murmured.

"We're partners now, remember? You come to my championship fights and sit in my corner, I go with you on these trips." He kissed the tip of her nose. "As long as you remember one thing, my lovely night shadow."

"What's that?"

He held her tight, his eyes possessive and full of love. "The only man you hunt from now on is me."

She nodded, her heart overflowing. "I've hunted for you all my life, Simon. You're the only man I want or need. No more shadows for me." Just sunshine, happiness, and love.

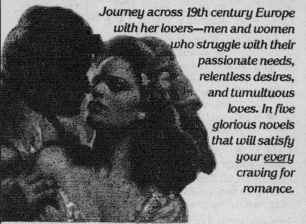

LAURA LONDON

Let her magical romances enchant you with their tenderness.

For glorious storytelling at its very best, get lost in these Regency romances.

___	A HEART TOO PROUD	13498-6	$2.95
___	THE BAD BARON'S DAUGHTER	10735-0	2.95
___	THE GYPSY HEIRESS	12960-5	2.95
___	LOVE'S A STAGE	15387-5	2.95
___	MOONLIGHT MIST	15464-4	2.95

All-new
**Candlelight
Newsletter**

**An exceptional,
free offer awaits readers
of Dell's incomparable Candlelight Ecstasy and Supreme Romances.**

Subscribe to our all-new CANDLELIGHT NEWSLETTER and you will receive—at absolutely no cost to you—exciting, exclusive information about today's finest romance novels and novelists. You'll be part of a select group to receive sneak previews of upcoming Candlelight Romances, well in advance of publication.

You'll also go behind the scenes to "meet" our Ecstasy and Supreme authors, learning firsthand where they get their ideas and how they made it to the top. News of author appearances and events will be detailed, as well. And contributions from the Candlelight editor will give you the inside scoop on how she makes her decisions about what to publish—and how *you* can try your hand at writing an Ecstasy or Supreme.

You'll find all this and more in Dell's CANDLELIGHT NEWSLETTER. And best of all, *it costs you nothing*. That's right! It's Dell's way of thanking our loyal Candlelight readers and of adding another dimension to your reading enjoyment.

Just fill out the coupon below, return it to us, and look forward to receiving the first of many CANDLELIGHT NEWSLETTERS—overflowing with the kind of excitement that only enhances our romances!

**DELL READERS SERVICE—DEPT. B925D
P.O. BOX 1000, PINE BROOK, N.J. 07058**

Name_____

Address_____

City_____

State_____ Zip_____